"I hate you," Claudia whispered

"No you don't," Cesare contradicted. "You hate the truth. You're fascinated by me. You always have been. Exactly as I always have been fascinated by you."

She looked up at him with eyes that were soft and frightened. She could feel the pulses leaping at her throat and wrists, as though she were about to faint. "Let me go."

"Not a chance," he murmured. "You've been in my blood a long time, Claudia. You're the most beautiful woman I've ever seen in my life!"

His eyes were gray pools, not cold as she'd once thought, but warm, warm and passionate.

"This whole thing is crazy," she heard a voice say with cool clarity, and realized it was her own. "Let me go, please."

MADELEINE KER is a self-described "compulsive writer." In fact, Madeleine has been known to deliver six romances in less than a year. She is married and lives in Spain.

Books by Madeleine Ker

MADELEINE KER

KER

tuscan encounter

Harlequin Books

TORONTO • NEW YORK • LONDON
AMSTERDAM • PARIS • SYDNEY • HAMBURG
STOCKHOLM • ATHENS • TOKYO • MILAN

Harlequin Presents first edition March 1990
ISBN 0-373-11249-1

Original hardcover edition published in 1988
by Mills & Boon Limited

CHAPTER ONE

'DI STEFANO is a powerful man, Claudia! Taking him on is no laughing matter.'

Vittorio Brunelli, her black-haired, black-eyed fiancé of four months' standing, sent her one of the flashing glances that always made her heart turn over.

'He doesn't scare me, Vito,' Claudia smiled. 'I've met him a dozen times, and he's absolutely charming. A decadent aristocrat, and definitely a lady-killer, but hardly a monster.' She tapped the lawyer's letter. 'This whole thing is a farrago of dukes and parchments and ancient popes. Di Stefano knows it's a bluff. He's just trying it on!'

'Don't fool yourself,' Vittorio said. 'He's not an ordinary man. He doesn't "try things on". He's far from decadent, either, though he likes to give the impression that he is. In fact, he is rich and powerful, and that means a lot in this part of Italy.'

'I'm not exactly poor, either,' she reminded him, folding slender arms.

'You're a lot poorer than Cesare di Stefano,' Vito said drily. 'Besides which, your case is a lot weaker.'

Claudia snorted. 'Oh, come on! Will any judge take that faded old scrap of parchment seriously?'

Vito shrugged elegantly. 'Faded old scraps of parchment matter in Italian law. And this one bears a pope's signature.'

'It's a historical document, with curiosity value,'

she retorted. 'For God's sake, the sixteenth century is over!'

'You think the sixteenth century is over?' Vito slipped his thumbs into the waistcoat pockets of his beautiful charcoal suit, and gave her a sinister look. 'Just take a look out of the window. Go on, take a look!'

To please her fiancé, Claudia walked over to the window of his office, and looked out at the small Tuscan town of Ferraro. She could see what he meant, of course. The place didn't belong to the twentieth century at all.

That it was twilight made the scene all the more evocative. The tower of the Church of San Felipe rose above a sea of ancient tiled roofs, stark against the pellucid sky. Beyond it, the lesser spires of cypresses and pines rose up here and there among the immemorial olive groves that surrounded the town. From the chartered accountant's office where Vittorio worked, you could see into the town square, which had been built in 1493 by Maurizio di Stefano, the third Duke of Ferraro, for the specific purpose—so Vittorio claimed—of executing his enemies.

Just to add to the theatricality of it all, it was the dead moment between the dinner hour and lighting-up time. Not a car was to be seen in the narrow streets, with arched Renaissance windows and elaborately carved wooden doors crowding on either side of the streets, and not a lamplight glimmered in the dusk.

By the time the townspeople came out into the streets for their early evening *passeggiata*, the lights would be bright, and the shop windows would be gleaming with edible and non-edible goodies. But right now, the town was lost in the mists of its own antiquity. Claudia had to make a conscious effort not to be impressed by that dark presence.

'Don't forget,' Vito broke into her thoughts, 'that a di Stefano practically built this town, four hundred years ago. Nineteen generations of them are buried in that church you're looking at. And that square outside is drenched in the blood spilled by those nineteen previous dukes.'

'Oh, I *love* that bit. Melodrama suits you, Vito.' She turned her back on the town, and smiled at him. Claudia Brennan's hair was the deep, rich red of a copper beech, and she was very beautiful. She had the kind of radiance which revealed her intelligence at once. It wasn't just a matter of fine bone-structure, magnificent hair, and a gorgeous, mobile mouth—though she had all three. It was also something that sparkled in her green eyes, something that animated her features and gave her a kind of crystalline glow.

Most men would have considered Vittorio Brunelli a very lucky young man. Unconventional and impulsive though she might be, Claudia was a ravishingly attractive woman, and she had the kind of looks and character that would continue to be luminous well into old age.

When she smiled at men, they nearly always smiled back, even if she'd just snatched a parking place—or a tempting piece of business—from under their noses. But Vittorio Brunelli didn't smile back on this occasion.

'I'm not trying to be funny,' he said. 'I'm serious.'

'So what are you saying?' she challenged. 'That Cesare di Stefano is going to have me hanged in the town square?'

'The di Stefano preference was for crucifixion,' Vito said succinctly. Claudia couldn't help a slight shudder. 'I'm saying that they have a very finely developed faculty of looking after what is theirs, and are quite used to fighting—and winning. Of all the landowners in Tuscany, you had to get involved with *him*,' Vito went on, shaking his dark head. 'I wish to God you'd consulted me before you bought that farm, Claudia.'

'You were in Switzerland,' she reminded him.

'You should have waited until I'd got back. Or at least called me.'

'It was going to be a surprise,' she sighed. 'And they had another buyer. If I hadn't come up with the money *pronto,* they'd have sold it to someone else.'

'Claudia, Claudia . . .' Vittorio pinched his nose tiredly. 'They always say that. Didn't you know? Haven't I warned you about this kind of thing often enough? You're supposed to have such a good head for business. This just goes to prove my point that women are too gullible to be really good in business——'

'Yes, I know what your point is,' she interrupted. 'But I thought it was an acceptable gamble to take. I still think it was an acceptable gamble to have taken.'

'Did you really expect that Cesare di Stefano would let his tenants sell you seventeen acres of his property? That he would just shrug and smile?'

'But it's *not* his property,' Claudia said briskly. 'That's just the thing. According to the law, the Rossis owned the property.'

'It seems thay did not.'

'They did. Oh, I know what di Stefano's little

game is, Vito—it's as clear as day! That land had devolved to the Rossis years ago, and as far as di Stefano was concerned, it was lost to his estate, with no chance of getting it back. But now that it's been sold to a rich foreigner, he or his lawyers have seen a cunning chance of getting it back again. At my expense! *That's* what this is all about. But my title to the land is impregnable. Legally speaking, everything was perfectly above board.'

'Buying property is never above board in Italy,' Vito said impatiently. 'Especially not in Tuscany. The set of land laws you're talking about happen to be extremely complicated in their application. I'm an accountant, for God's sake. I know. As it is, we'll be lucky to get any of that money back from the Rossis.'

Claudia tightened her mouth. 'I don't want the money back, Vito. I want that farm. It's mine.'

Vito's handsome face set into a look she had come to know very well. Privately, she called it his now-look-here-my-good-little-woman look. 'Claudia, you've got to understand one thing right now. The only way out of this mess——' He held up a lean hand to emphasise his point. '—the *only* way out—is to sue the Rossis for the money you paid them. Trying to hold on to the farm means taking on di Stefano. And that I would strongly advise you not to attempt.'

Claudia turned away. 'I want that farm,' she repeated with an obstinate set of the mouth.

'But why? It's just a tumbledown farmstead, like ten thousand others in this province!'

'It's beautiful. And I want it!'

Vito tried to sound patient. 'This isn't a time for being sentimental, Claudia—either about that farm, or about di Stefano. His threats are not idle. He can employ the sort of lawyers who'll eat you for breakfast, and if he doesn't feel like spending that much money, he can always just have you dropped into the Arno, with concrete boots on.'

'You should have been an actor,' she said in mockery. 'The way your eyebrows come down like that is quite chilling. And concrete boots! That's positively 1930s Chicago.'

Vito ignored her derision. 'Anyway, personally, I don't think you stand a chance in court.'

'Why not? The law's the law, and apart from that ridiculous bit of parchment, he doesn't even have any proper deeds.'

'Nor do you,' Vittorio pointed out.

'But *legally*,' she insisted, 'I'm in the right. That's what the lawyer in Pisa said.'

'You could be,' Vito nodded. 'But proving that you're in the right is quite another matter. Trying to convince some judge that the property belonged to the Rossis, and not to di Stefano, will be very expensive, very time-consuming, and very complicated. The lawyer also told you *that*, didn't he?'

'Yes,' Claudia admitted. 'But he was willing to take the case on.'

'Of course he was,' Vito agreed cynically. 'He woud be assured of years of profitable employment at your expense, wouldn't he? You know very well that it can take a long, long time in Italy before a civil case even gets to court.'

'How long?'

'I know people who've been waiting a decade.'

'Ten *years?* And we won't be able to use the house all that time?'

'Do I have to keep reminding you? You're not in

England. Things are different here, very different.'

'You're telling me!'

Vito pulled a bottle of whisky out of a drawer, and poured himself a drink. He didn't offer Claudia one; she never drank anything but wine. Her palate was too valuable.

'There's something else,' he went on, turning the glass in his fingers. 'Possession is nine-tenths of the law. And he has possession, not you. That makes his case twice as strong to start with. Suing the Rossis for the money is feasible. Suing di Stefano for the land is not. I assure you, my dear, that however charming you may have found him in the past, he is not a man to tangle with. He's as slippery as a wolf.'

'Wolves aren't slippery,' she pointed out.

'Well, he's as slippery as a stiletto between the ribs, then.' The young accountant—he was only five years older than Claudia herself, who was twenty-five—drained his whisky at a gulp, Italian-style. 'Do you think I'm exaggerating?'

'Exaggerating?' Her eyes lost their focus for a moment as she thought of Cesare di Stefano. He was one of the few men she knew who was actually better-looking than Vito. He was, in fact, a stunningly handsome man, with the charming manners and cultured speech of the true aristocrat. She remembered clear, deep grey eyes, emphasised by thick black lashes and rather heavy lids, and a devastatingly sexy mouth that seemed to wear a continual smile, as though life and everything in it—especially women—amused him greatly.

It was the sort of dangerous combination that always sent her weak at the knees. But she didn't see him as a really serious enemy. And as for dropping people in the Arno——

'When you talk about concrete boots and stilettos, I think you're raving,' she agreed at last. 'He's not like that at all. He's a warm, colourful personality, and I've always liked the man. I thought he liked me.'

'Maybe a bit too much,' Vito grunted. 'I can guarantee one thing, though: no matter how much he enjoys flirting with you, he'll be as ruthless with you over this land as though you were his worst enemy. Claudia, listen to me! Forget the farm. If we tackle the Rossis head-on, there's just a chance that they'll cough up the money, or at least most of it, without too much of a struggle. Be guided by me for once in your life.'

'I'm always guided by you,' she sighed.

Vito's beautifully tapered eyebrows descended in an expression of dissatisfaction. 'Unfortunately, that isn't true. You're too impulsive, Claudia. You take chances. Your behaviour is intuitive, mercurial. Typically feminine, in other words.'

'Here we go,' Claudia murmured, rolling her eyes heavenward.

'For a woman,' Vito went on magisterially, 'you have done exceptionally well. No one can deny that. Sometimes those creative, intuitive decisions pay off. You know your business, I grant you that, too. But in the long run, steadiness and constancy win out over intuition, no matter how clever it is. This mistake over the farm just proves my point. My love, there comes a time in every woman's life when she begins to need a man's stability. A time when she knows she must hand over the reins to a man. And I believe that this time has come for you, now.'

'I know you do.' Against his dark good looks—he had the olive skin and brilliant eyes of the true

Mediterranean type—and his more sober character, Claudia's wayward Englishness took on an added brightness. Right now, her eyes were like gems, bright and clear, an indication of intense mental activity.

Vito came from a large family, in which, true to local tradition, the males were pampered and spoiled by the females from infancy to old age. In return, they were expected to handle every aspect of family business.

Since his father's death, he had been the head of his family, deferred to and held in awe by the numerous womenfolk. He had done the right thing by them. And Vito was unshakeably convinced of his duty to protect Claudia in exactly the same way—even if being her custodian also meant taking away much of the liberty she prized so highly.

His views on women were prehistoric by her standards. She'd have found them infuriating long ago, if they hadn't amused her. In fact, she still took a naughty delight in shocking him with her independent views on marriage, divorce, working women, and chauvinistic men. He was, of course, very easily shocked, which was maybe part of the fun.

The difference was that he was serious, even though she might not be. Yet, perversely, although it affronted her, that chauvinism also drew her like a magnet. Whatever the truth was, it lay at the heart of her relationship with Vito Brunelli—a powerful attraction of opposites.

'Anyway,' Claudia said, dismissing the subject for the time being, 'we were talking about my farm. So he's got possession, and lawsuits can take ten years. But I want my vineyards, Vittorio, and I'm not giving up without a struggle. So what are you suggesting?'

He leaned back in his chair, his glass poised in one hand. 'I'm suggesting that *you* keep right out of it. You've done enough damage as it is.'

'Oh, thank you very much.'

'Just sit tight. And forget about that farm. In the meantime, I'll talk it over with Piero and my uncles. The first thing is to approach the Rossis privately, and see what can be done. There might be a way out of this mess that avoids going to court.' He gave her a warning glance. 'But it may cost you money.'

Claudia sighed. 'I don't particularly want your brother and your loud-mouthed uncles to take my problem over for me.'

'They're more of a match for the Rossis than you are, at any rate,' Vittorio said shortly. He replaced his glass and whisky bottle in the drawer, and looked up at her. 'Know what my basic conclusion about this whole mess is?' he asked.

'Go on,' she invited. 'Surprise me.'

He smiled for the first time that afternoon, showing attractive white teeth. 'No matter how clever she may be, no matter how experienced she may be, a woman in business will eventually, inevitably, take a fall. And then some man will have to fish her out.'

On the way back to Pisa, Claudia was feeling distinctly irritable with Vito, and not just because of that last, uncalled-for remark. She was disappointed with his whole attitude. Sometimes she absolutely detested that patronising tone of his. Whatever mistakes she'd made, she expected him to be rather more loyal and supportive in her time of need.

But what really got to her was the streak of mean satisfaction she detected in him—satisfaction that things had gone wrong, proving that women really weren't fit to make big decisions.

When Vito spoke of 'handing over the reins', he meant exactly that. He meant that, once they were married, he expected to take over the business she had singlehandedly built up, and run it himself. He'd made it quite clear that he wanted to exercise sole control over all their financial affairs once they were Mr and Mrs.

Wasn't that the most galling thing she'd ever heard in her life?

Well . . . yes and no. There was something about the now-look-here-my-good-little-woman approach that exerted an odd fascination over her. Maybe it was because inwardly she felt he was right—that she *had* been extraordinarily lucky in getting her business this far, and that her luck couldn't hold out for ever. Maybe it was because somewhere in her soul, despite all appearances, lay a good-little-woman who secretly delighted in the thought of being looked after by a husky man like Vito.

After all, most of the women she knew, including herself, had been brought up with an inbuilt lack of confidence in themselves versus men.

Women with guts, of course, overcame it, and ended up doing better than any man. That was the path she herself had chosen. But inside her there was always that dangerous pull to go the other way. To give up the struggle, and just enjoy life, letting the authoritative male take over for her.

Vito was exactly that. She'd met him eighteen months ago, through her business. Coming to the Chianti region several times a year, as she'd been doing since she was twenty, and travelling quite extensively to buy wine for her Highbury shops, she'd needed an accountant's help from time to time, and Vito had been recommended by a mutual contact.

They'd been intrigued by one another from the start. At first, it had been more negative than positive. He'd found her too independent, too outspoken, and far too bossy for a woman. She, on the other hand, had been fascinated by him as a prime example of the kind of handsome chauvinist male she most disliked.

But the attraction had been there from the first. Claudia, who had never known a father, found herself almost enjoying the way Vito cosseted her, lectured her, worried over her, and generally tried to dominate her; and Vito clearly relished the fiction that he was 'taming' his skittish English beauty.

Given their mutual antagonism, the fact that both were physically very attractive people, and that work brought them into regular contact with each other, it was perhaps inevitable that their relationship had blossomed into a romance, the kind of sudden romance that often grows between people who are very different in character.

There was also, of course, Claudia's love of Tuscany to take into consideration. Her dream of a Tuscan farmhouse had been there for years. The rolling hills and rich vineyards of Tuscany had got into her blood a long time ago, something which had perhaps predisposed her to fall in love with someone of this earth.

When Vittoria had proposed, four months ago, that they get married, and set up a home in Tuscany, something had clicked inside her. She'd actually heard it click, like a tumbler falling into place. There had been no hesitation in her 'yes'.

Not that either family had been exactly thrilled. Her mother hated the thought of Claudia living in a foreign country; and his family, poor things, were alarmed by her liberated manners and life-style.

But the obvious happiness of Claudia and Vittorio had silenced any protests from the Brennan and Brunelli families.

The idea had been that they find an old farmhouse with a bit of land in the Chianti region, 'ripe for restoration', as the estate agents put it. They would use Claudia's money to buy it. Vittorio's uncle, an architect, would design them a lovely home in the old shell. He had other relations who would undertake the building work.

She would—according to Vito, at any rate—then delegate the running of her London shops to her new husband, and they would settle down to a blissful life in the sun.

The only question was how far she was going to be tamed. Or going to pretend to be tamed. Was she really going to hand over to Vito, and become the placid Italian wife? She hadn't made her mind up yet. And Vito knew it, which was why he lost no opportunity in pointing out how weak a single woman's position was in the world. This business over the farm, of course, had given him several years' supply of ammunition.

She, as always, would argue back. But, no matter how she loved her work, there was a looming question she knew she'd eventually have to face, for she also wanted Vito, and she wanted children, and she knew that she couldn't have all three at the same time.

Once they had a house, she felt sure, everything would somehow work out. She'd seen it all in her mind's eye. The House Beautiful, a home for them and their burgeoning family. Leaving England's rainy climate behind her for most of the year. Coming to some acceptable compromise with her husband about work. Long summer's days spent wandering blissfully among her own vines. A few thousand bottles of her own vintage each year, with her own name on the label. Being able to recommend a bottle or two to very special customers.

This is my own stuff. We've got a little place near Lucca, just a few acres, but the stock is quite good. I think you'll like it . . .

Vittorio had just left for Switzerland when a farmer she dealt with had let drop, quite casually, that a good vineyard was up for sale outside Lucca. She'd driven out to see the place the next day. It was perfect. A lovely old farmhouse needing renovation, bordered with pine groves and two or three small olive orchards. All around it, terraces of ancient vines, with wildflowers blooming between the rows, and a wonderful view of the medieval town of Lucca.

Just thinking about it now in the car made her sigh dreamily.

The Rossis didn't have any deeds. That was not altogether rare in this very rural part of Tuscany. However, their family had been renting the land from a much larger estate since the beginning of the century. They had documents to prove it and, according to modern Italian law, that gave them the right to sell the land to a third party. So Claudia believed, anyway. The notary, with whom she'd checked the Rossis' title to the land, had agreed that there should be no problems. It was unlikely that the original landlords even remembered that the land existed.

When the Rossis had started pressing her, saying that another buyer was ready to sign the contract that very week, she'd put down a *compromesso*, binding herself to buy the property. As was the way in Tuscany, the whole sale had been completed quickly, and within a few days, in fact, she'd paid over the full amount.

Vito's family, when she'd triumphantly broken the news, had not been as delighted as she might have expected. Their reaction had been distinctly cool. At first she'd put that down to their being rather shocked that she, a woman, should have taken such a major step without consulting her fiancé.

And then, the crunch.

A formal lawyer's letter—hand-written, not typed, in a crabbed archaic hand—informing her that the property she'd bought from the Rossis actually belonged to His Excellency Cesare Massimo di Stefano, the twentieth Duke of Ferraro, who possessed an ancient title over it, granted to him by Pope Urban III in 1791. A photocopy of the document was enclosed. And would she please refrain from trespassing on the property any further, or else an injunction would be obtained to evict her.

After decades of having forgotten that the farm existed at all, the Duke was suddenly holding on to what was his own.

As he was a major wine-producer of the area, she'd naturally met di Stefano several times over the past couple of years. It was something of a shock to find herself suddenly at daggers drawn with the man.

But, since she'd started buying Chianti wines and

importing them to England four years ago, she'd got to know the Tuscan character well. Any woman, especially a moneyed, foreign woman, tended to be fair game in their eyes. No doubt di Stefano thought she would be intimidated enough to surrender all rights to the farm forthwith; which in turn would mean the restoration of the property, with vacant possession, to the di Stefano estate. And this was a property which had legally ceased to belong to the estate almost fifty years ago!

Oh, yes, it was a clever ploy. She ought to have been warned by that Dick Turpin sparkle in the deep grey eyes of His Excellency, the Duke of Ferraro.

Well, she was blowed if she was going to stand and deliver. Direct retaliatory action was needed, now.

Why not go and see Cesare di Stefano in person? That would give her some idea of the man's intentions, at least. Hope flickered inside her as the idea blossomed. Maybe she and di Stefano could talk sensibly about this. If she could impress him that she was serious about fighting for the vineyards, he might not be so keen to face a court case.

At the very least, she might negotiate some kind of compromise—say, a deal involving her buying more di Stefano wine. Maybe even a split of the property. Anyway, something a long way short of surrender.

That would show Vito, *and* his loud-mouthed uncles, whom she detested, that a woman could do business, after all!

She got to the Splendid by seven-thirty. Despite the name, it really was a splendid hotel, and worlds away from the shabby little *pensione* where she used to stay during her first buying trips. She occasionally stayed with Vittorio's family on her visits, but actually preferred the hotel. It was expensive, but it gave her the freedom she was used to, and above all, privacy—which didn't exist in the crowded and very noisy Brunelli household.

She parked the hired car in the car park, and walked into the marble-halled reception.

'I won't bother with dinner tonight,' she told the clerk. 'Could I have a salad in my room in half an hour, please? And can you get me a number?'

'Naturally, *Signorina* Brennan. What name?'

'Cesare di Stefano, Duke of Ferraro. Put the call through to my room—when you've got him on the line.' She thought for a moment. 'Don't bother unless it's the Duke himself. I don't want to talk to his staff.'

'Of course, *signorina,*' the receptionist beamed, looking impressed.

Claudia smiled to herself as she stepped into the lift. Start as you mean to go on. That was what Daddy had always said. She was quite looking forward to a little conversation with His Excellency.

She was just kicking off her shoes when the bedside phone chirruped.

'The Duke is on the line,' the receptionist announced in an awe-stricken tone. 'I'm putting you through.'

'Thanks.' Claudia sat cross-legged on the bed, her eyes bright, and waited. The familiar voice, deep and smooth, came on the line.

'Good evening,' he said in English.

'Good evening, Your Excellency. It's Claudia Brennan speaking, in connection with the property near Lucca.'

'Ah, yes,' the voice purred. 'How nice to hear from you, *cara*. An unfortunate misunderstanding. Still, these things happen.'

'There's no misunderstanding,' Claudia said briskly. 'Not, at least, between me and the former owners of the property.'

'The former owners of the property were the Dukes of Milan.' It was delivered as an interesting piece of information, not as a rebuke. 'But that was only until 1791, when they fell out with Pope Urban III over some matter of a few thousand ducats. Or was it 1792? In any case, the land came into the hands of my family at about that time. I myself am the present owner.'

'I would contest that,' she retorted.

'That is your privilege,' he said, 'though a somewhat idiosyncratic one.'

'Your Excellency, I bought that property on the open market——'

'You are mistaken,' he cut through with unruffled calm. 'You gave a large sum of money to two persons who happened to be renting the property, but who had no right to sell it. That does not constitute a purchase.'

'It does in this case,' she pursued, starting to be annoyed by the smooth, mocking way he was treating her. 'Those people had been living on the farm for several generations. The only rent they paid was in wine and olive oil. Under Italian law, that gives them complete possession of the property, including the right to sell it. To my mind, the sale is perfectly legal.'

'Alas,' the regret was as smooth as his own Chianti, 'you will find otherwise. But please don't think I am without sympathy for you. After all, we are friends, are we not?'

'I'd like to think so.' She had a quick vision of those wickedly assessing grey eyes.

'Exactly. Yours is indeed a melancholy situation. Unfortunately, I am attended by a dozen dinner guests at this very moment. I quite understand that you wish to unburden yourself to someone, but I really cannot just abandon my old acquaintances . . .'

'Very well,' she said, keeping down her anger, 'but I insist that we meet to discuss this!'

'Why, yes.' He sounded charmed by the idea. 'That would be most pleasant. Where did you have in mind?'

'My lawyer's office in Pisa.'

'Too sordid for words,' he said decisively. 'You must come to the *palazzo*. You can give me your opinion of this year's vintage—I value your expert opinion most highly.'

'It won't be a social occasion,' she said, her voice sandpaper to his velvet. 'We're going to have to face facts, Your Excellency, or this will all end up in a very messy and expensive court case.'

'Expensive, yes. For you. But messy, no. The ownership of the property is not in the slightest doubt.'

'The judge will have to decide *that!*'

There was a sigh. 'My dear Miss Brennan, you might as well take your own sovereign to court, claiming that a Cockney street vendor outside Buckingham Palace had sold you the whole property, Beefeaters included.'

'The Beefeaters are at the Tower,' she said with childish spite. 'The ones at Buckingham Palace are the Palace Guards.'

'Indeed?' Not a note in the deep, rich timbre had been disturbed by her anger. 'How interesting. I find your English traditions and customs most intriguing.'

'Well, we have a tradition and custom of fighting for what is ours,' she told him grimly. 'You'll find that I'm not a fool to be brushed off so lightly!'

'But of course,' he said silkily. 'Let me see. Why not come for a week or two in November? The shooting is rough, but if you're a good shot you ought to get a decent bag.'

'*November?*'

'Yes. Or perhaps you don't shoot?'

Claudia gritted her teeth. This kind of mockery would be amusing, if there weren't tens of thousands of pounds at stake. 'This is June, Your Excellency,' she reminded him acidly. 'We need to talk about this at once! I have to be back in London by the end of the month. Can we meet some time over the next few days?'

'Ah. That might be difficult. I have so much to do, you see.'

'So have I,' Claudia pointed out irritably. 'What's wrong with Friday?'

'On Friday I am entertaining my Great-Aunt Adele, the Duchess of Padua,' he mused. 'Unfortunately, she detests strangers. A quirk of her advanced age—she is almost one hundred.'

Claudia, starting to understand that this man was playing with her, and that keeping her cool was the only way to play back, waited patiently.

'But she will probably be asleep by four,' he mused. 'In which case she will be spared the annoyance of having to meet a young, foreign, and beautiful stranger—and you will be spared her interminable reminiscences of the last century. Now that I come to think of it, it has been a long time since I enjoyed your company—and that wonderful red hair. What about an *English tea?*' he concluded, with a air of gracious condescension, as though it were some slightly juvenile eccentricity he would stoop to for her sake. 'Yes. We shall have one in your honour. Join me Friday afternoon at four?'

'Very well.'

'But you must not call me "Your Excellency". We know each other too well by now. Besides, it makes me sound like a colonial governor, and I assure you that is most inappropriate. *Signor* will do perfectly well.'

'If you say so,' Claudia replied drily.

'By the way, I have often meant to ask you,' he enquired, 'do you by any chance have Italian blood? Claudia is an Italian name.'

He had pronounced it in the Latin way, as though it were 'cloudier'. For some reason, that irritated her. Even the Brunellis made the effort to pronounce her name the way she preferred it, corresponding to the Italian 'Clodia'.

'Actually, it's Claudia,' she said stiffly, giving it the English pronunciation, 'and I have no Italian blood.'

'Ah,' he said regretfully, as though she'd confessed to some unfortunate defect. ' "There was a young lady called Claudia, whose behaviour grew steadily bawdier." I prefer the Italian pronunciation. "There was a young lady called *Claudia,* whose appearance grew steadily *dowdier* . . ." There. I'm afraid neither limerick looks like reaching a flattering conclusion. Until Friday, then.'

'Until Friday,' she agreed numbly, and heard the receiver click in her ear.

CHAPTER TWO

VITO almost choked over his wine. *'What?'* he blinked. 'Why? When did you arrange this?'

'Last night. Thank you, Alfredo.' The diminutive waiter of the equally diminutive *trattoria* had brought them their lunch. Veal cutlets for Vito, and a cheese salad for herself. Claudia picked at the fresh green stuff while she went on, 'He wants me to join him for afternoon tea, no less. But I have to be careful to avoid his Great-Aunt Adele, the Duchess of Padua, who is a hundred years old, and detests strangers.' She smiled. 'Was he just pulling my leg, d'you think?'

'I wouldn't know,' Vittorio said shortly. 'I don't mix in his circles.' He scowled at her before tackling his veal. 'You really are the limit, sometimes. What on earth do you expect to get out of him?'

'I don't quite know,' she admitted. After last night's conversation, she'd felt rather like a mouse who had just been batted about between a cat's paws. She'd been a game to him. It had occurred to her to doubt whether there was really any point to going to see him for his 'English tea'; the formidable intellect behind that smoothly teasing manner was as well hidden as the steel hand inside the velvet glove. But it was there, all right. Another game of verbal hide-and-seek with the handsome *signor* was very obviously on the cards. 'I just hoped I could talk things over with him, and reach some compromise.'

'You mean you hope you'll be able to beguile him

into parting with seventeen acres by fluttering your eyelashes?' Vito snorted. 'Your charms may be seductive, Claudia, but I assure that di Stefano is not that stupid.'

'Actually, I had something a little more sophisticated in mind,' Claudia said stiffly.

'Oh?' Vito's eyes glittered. 'I hope that doesn't mean what I think it means.'

'Don't be disgusting,' she snapped. 'Your trouble is that you can't see past the fact that I'm a woman. I intend to talk business with di Stefano, nothing more.'

Vito just grunted, and lowered his eyes. It was Claudia who broke the awkward pause again.

'How's your veal?' she asked.

'Overcooked,' Vito said irritably, pushing away his plate with a frown.

Claudia picked out a piece of *ricotta* cheese and offered it to him placatingly. 'Are you really angry with me?'

'I'm angry that you never listen to my advice,' he growled. 'I told you not to get involved any further, and you've disobeyed me. What kind of marriage are we going to have if you insist on doing everything without consulting me?'

'A very happy marriage,' she soothed.

'Not at this rate! I presume you expect me to accompany you on Friday?'

'No, thanks,' she said sweetly. 'You weren't invited.'

'You don't want me with you?' he said incredulously.

'It's not that,' she smiled. 'But you have to realise that there are some things I must see through myself. This is my mess, as you so kindly pointed out last night. Besides,' she went on, 'I can't just surrender every responsibility to you. We aren't even married yet. And in any case, I know him better than you do. I think it would be much better if I dealt with this on my own.'

'I see,' he glared.

'Come on,' she cajoled, 'what harm can it do to go and speak to the man?'

'Plenty,' Vittorio said hotly. 'It shows no propriety.'

'Propriety! What's propriety got to do with anything?'

'More than you imagine! I would have thought you'd learned your lesson by now, Claudia. The more you get involved with di Stefano, the worse off you'll be. I really wish you wouldn't just *do* things, without thinking over the consequences, without referring to me first . . .'

'This is the last time, I promise. If I can't do any good on Friday, you can have a free hand.'

'When we're married——'

'When we're married, I'll be a good, docile Italian wife. Just wait and see. I won't spend a penny or say a word to anyone without consulting you.'

'Then why don't you want me with you tomorrow?'

'Because we're not married yet,' she retorted. He glowered over his food, obviously angry with her. Male pride, she reflected, was an odd thing—easily wounded, difficult to patch up when deflated. But she still hadn't quite forgiven him for his attitude last night. This would show him that she wasn't quite in the bag yet!

She smiled to herself, and crunched a piece of lettuce. Keeping slim was a full-time occupation in

Italy. How did Italian women manage, given all the temptations?

'Very well,' Vito said heavily at the end of the meal, 'I suppose I must give my consent.'

Claudia had to hide a smile. Vito knew perfectly well that his consent was irrelevant. But she played up to him for the sake of his Italian pride.

'Thank you,' she said gravely.

'Just remember,' he said grimly, 'that he is in the position of strength, not you.'

'I will,' she promised. 'I'll be very careful.'

As always, Vito paid the bill. He wouldn't have dreamed of letting her do it. She was going to be busy that afternoon, dealing with her shippers in Pisa. She told him so, and asked, 'Shall I see you tomorrow?'

He shook his head brusquely. 'I doubt there'll be time. I've got too much work to do.' It was said coldly enough to let her know that this was her punishment for rejecting his help. She gave a mental shrug.

'I've got plenty of things to attend to myself,' she said easily. 'Let's have a drink on Friday evening, at my hotel, when I get back from di Stefano. If I'm still alive, that is,' she smiled.

'Very well,' he agreed with ill grace.

'Maybe we'll have something to celebrate! Don't work too hard. And don't worry about me and di Stefano. I'm not as big a fool as you think I am.'

Their farewells were not exactly warm, but Claudia had no intentions of letting Vito beat her on this point. Let him sulk if he wished; it was important that she kept showing him she intended to keep plenty of control over her own affairs—otherwise the outlook for their married life was hardly rosy!

Despite Vittorio being cross with her, she was feeling a lot more cheerful today. Claudia thrived on challenges. She was always far happier struggling against odds than plodding along in the same old routine.

That was the way she'd always been. Some women who are born beautiful find life very easy; with Claudia it had been the reverse. Right through childhood, school and two years of college, she'd always taken what her mother called 'the path of greatest resistance'.

She'd had few advantages in life. Claudia had never known her father, who had died when she was a babe in arms, and she'd always keenly felt that lack of a guiding male presence in her childhood.

Her mother had never remarried, and the pension she and Claudia had lived on was barely adequate. She hadn't known poverty, but she had never known real financial security, either.

That was why she had never minded struggling for success in business.

In her teens, she'd started working in a local restaurant, run by an Italian couple who imported limited quantities of Chianti wine to complement the fine Tuscan cuisine they provided. It hadn't escaped Claudia's notice that the customers, without fail, adored the wines. So many of them wanted to buy bottles to take home that she grew heartily sick of the litany she had to repeat—'Sorry, the manager only imports a small quantity of wine, and he never sells individual bottles to customers.'

That was when she'd first got the idea.

Amused by her curiosity, the manager had encouraged her to taste and judge the wines for herself, teaching her discriminate between those that were adequate, and those that were superb. Over the two years she'd worked there, she'd learned a great deal.

A holiday to Italy when she was seventeen had confirmed three things—that she loved Tuscany, that she loved Italian food and wine, and that her idea was viable.

She'd taught herself to speak fluent Italian in a few weeks, and she'd even taught herself to speak that much more difficult language, the wine-expert's jargon.

Of course, it didn't help that the career she'd chosen was a field traditionally dominated by men. She'd had to fight prejudice against her sex and her youth. And she'd had to work harder than she'd ever dreamed possible.

Despite her instinct, bringing local Chianti wines, generally thought to be inferior to French burgundies and to travel badly, to the high streets of London, had been a gamble. But, like so many of Claudia Brennan's gambles, it had paid off. From the first ten cases she'd bought with her life's savings, and sold to Islington wine merchants a few streets from where she'd been born, Colefax & Brennan had been on the up and up.

There was, in fact, no Colefax, but the two names sounded prosperous, established and respectable. To buyers sceptical at her youth and beauty, she'd even hinted that Colefax existed—a cobwebby and reassuringly ancient male presence in the background. Someone whose judgement and palate you could trust.

After a year of almost casual importing, with a few failures and a lot of successes, she'd suddenly found herself with enough business to open a shop of her own.

On the drive through the vineyards, she thought about her impending interview with the Duke of Ferraro.

On the many occasions they'd met through business, she'd always been conscious of a spark between them. That special electric feeling you got with certain special men, the feeling that, given other circumstances, other places, more than friendship was possible . . .

Vito, with his sixth sense, had probably guessed that. He didn't really understand, though. Being engaged allowed you to enjoy that kind of sexy electricity without any fear of compromise. It had enhanced, rather than cramped, her enjoyment of di Stefano's company. Besides, she really had liked the man. He was cultured, suave and very amusing, and Claudia frankly relished male glamour. It was like good wine, something to be savoured on the palate.

Seeing him as an enemy, however, provoked very different reactions in her. She hadn't come this far to be plundered by some layabout aristocratic highwayman, no matter how charming, suave and handsome. She was going to fight!

She thought back to the telephone conversation they'd had. He'd made a primary mistake that evening. He'd revealed just how silly and weak he thought she was. Well, she was neither silly nor weak.

Maybe on Friday he'd make a few more mistakes. But she, for certain, would make none.

'Dogs are capable of loving a man far better than any woman. Don't you agree?'

Cesare di Stefano was fondling the silky ears of one of the hunting dogs that sat at his feet. The other was staring up at him adoringly. Claudia, seated opposite on the silk-covered *chaise* which was exquisitely uncomfortable, and had no doubt been selected for her for that very reason, smiled sourly.

'An interesting point. To get back to the property at Lucca——'

'Would you like some more tea?'

'No, thank you. My lawyer advises me that under

Italian law——'

'Or would you prefer coffee?'

'—the ownership of the property passed into the hands of the Rossis by right of continuous habitation——'

He passed her the wrought-silver dish. 'Have you tried these almond biscuits?'

'I don't want anything more to eat or drink,' she said in exasperation. 'Will you please listen to me?'

'But I am listening.' He smiled at her bewitchingly. Cesare di Stefano was as stunningly handsome as ever. His mouth, authoritative and sensual, was wearing its usual amused smile, and his eyes flattered her face and figure continually. The arching nostrils, and the lines that bracketed his mouth, however, spoke of arrogance and passion beneath the urbane surface, of darker emotions which until now she hadn't bothered to look for.

He was tall and lean, and dressed with supreme elegance in an English-style tweed suit. But he couldn't have looked less English. Tanned and somehow panther-like, he would have caused a sensation at any *real* English tea party. And no amount of good humour could disguise the dangerous quality that radiated from him, the way heat radiates from a fire. That, too, she hadn't noticed until today.

Looking at him now, it was a lot easier to believe in images like stilettos; this was a strong man, strong in both body and mind. The silvery wings in his otherwise jet-black hair suggested an age not far off forty, yet the way he moved, and the athletic grace of his body, contradicted any impression that he would be effete or decadent. He held the silver dish between long, supple fingers, as though it were a feather; she knew for a fact that it was immensely heavy. Those hands of his could crush as well as caress.

And yet he smiled and teased. And his voice was silky-smooth.

'I am listening with great interest, my dear Claudia,' he went on. He was still pronouncing it *cloudier*. 'What puzzles me, however, is how an intelligent woman like you, knowing something about Tuscany, can possibly believe in such an argument. That property has been in my family for two hundred years. By what right, then, can the Rossis possibly claim ownership?'

'There's no mystery about it, as you very well know,' she said impatiently. 'Legislation has been passed since your parchment of seventeen-whatever which gives tenants in agricultural areas the right to claim land which they've been working without pay. The Rossis have been working that land without pay for generations——'

'And without paying any rent,' he murmured, long lashes drooping over those beautiful grey eyes.

'Yes. That makes the situation all the clearer. They were working the land for nothing all those years, and they weren't paying any rent, either. Effectively, the land was theirs, and that piece of legislation confirms it.'

He shrugged elegantly with one shoulder, a gesture she remembered as quintessentially his. 'As with many of my tenants, the Rossis paid me in the form of produce—wine and olive oil. The fact that they never failed to pay that tithe, for generations, shows that they understood who really owned the land. I agree that if I had let them get away without paying for a decade or more, they might have some claim. But there are detailed records showing exactly what they paid each year.'

'Yes, but no *money* passed hands. That is the important thing!'

He considered her thoughtfully. 'Let me ask you something. Do you have any deeds for that property?'

'I have a bill of sale.' She looked at him squarely. 'Do *you* have any deeds?'

He smiled. 'I have my much-scorned parchment of seventeen-whatever.'

'I'm inclined to think that my bill of sale counts for more than your parchment,' she said with a gleam of triumph.

'That remains to be seen.'

The room they were sitting in overlooked the park; it was magnificently furnished, dominated by a huge crystal chandelier which hung from the stuccoed ceiling like a frozen fountain.

Vittorio had told her she'd know the house when she saw it; he'd been right. It was one of the finest examples of Florentine Palladian architecture she'd ever seen, set in an immense estate of great trees, with a lake over which, at its narrowest part, an arched stone bridge soared. The great vineyards stretched to the front of the house, almost to the horizon.

She'd known di Stefano was wealthy, but not *this* wealthy. It had been very hard—and it was still very hard—not to be overawed by the money and taste all around her. It seemed absurd to be haggling about a decrepit vineyard with a man who represented twenty generations of breeding, and whose ancestors stared at her from dozens of oil portraits all around the walls. Like him, many of them were darkly handsome. The expressions on their faces reflected power, arrogance, self-confidence.

He was watching her with something of that expression on his own face, now. The rather heavy lids were lowered over his eyes, and a slight smile still hung around the sensual curve of his mouth, but she felt, *knew*, that his attention was as focused as a hawk's.

'Let me ask you something else,' he said. 'What are your plans as regards this unfortunate matter?'

'That's what I've come to discuss with you.' She crossed her legs with a rustle of one silk-clad thigh against the other, and smoothed the fine linen skirt across her lap. It was an old gesture, one that meant she was getting down to business; di Stefano's grey eyes followed the movements of her hands, as though sharing the way they touched her body.

'As I've made quite clear,' she started briskly, 'I regard that property as my own. My first intention is to start restoring the house, which is in a ramshackle condition. When that's done, my fiancé and I will get married, and move into it. As our permanent home. We also intend to farm the vineyards. If you want to take legal action against us, then you are quite welcome to do so.' She gave him what she hoped was a confident smile. 'I shall certainly fight back, and I think I will win quite easily. I'm not afraid of a court case.'

'You show more bravery than sense,' he said gently. He was caressing the other dog now, long fingers moving in the glossy fur. 'Even if you win your case—which, if I may contradict you, is most unlikely—the costs are likely to come to far more than the property is worth.'

'In which case, you and I will both be out of pocket,' she pointed out, and paused. 'Unless we find some other way of settling our differences.'

His smile, if anything, widened. 'And what do you suggest?'

'Oh . . . I think we could come to some agreement.' She took a deep breath, but tried not to let it show. 'In consideration of your claim, I could let you have a part of the property—but not the house—which borders the rest of your land.'

'A part?' he repeated mildly.

'I'll go to four acres. But for that, I'll want your written undertaking that the rest of the property is mine, and mine alone.'

He leaned back, studying her with amusement. 'Let me get that clear. You are offering to give me four acres of my property—providing I let you steal the remaining thirteen?'

'I'm not stealing anything,' she flushed. 'The property is *mine*, and I consider my offer very generous.' She sat forward. 'I know what your strategy is, *signore*. I'm not a fool.'

'My strategy?'

'You see an easy way of getting back a property which had been lost to your estate years ago.' Her mouth tightened. 'But you'll find I'm not as soft a touch as you think. I intend to fight you every inch of the way.' She studied his face. 'Consider my offer, *signore*. It means the least loss of money for both of us. It means neither of us having to lose a fortune in legal fees.'

He made a dismissive gesture. 'Legal fees don't alarm me, my dear Claudia. I am hardly poor, as you can see.'

'Quite.' She looked round the room, which must contain tens of thousands of pounds' worth of artworks and antiques. 'That property probably means next to nothing to you. Is it really worth all the trouble and expense of a court case?'

'There will be no court case,' he said with impeccable logic, 'if you give up this absurd claim. As a matter of fact, I am screening new tenants for that property already. Besides . . .' The smile was pleasant.

'. . . it will be a simple matter to prosecute you, win my suit, and then sue you for my legal costs. Doing that would not cost me a *lira,* and would provide a great deal of innocent amusement for my lawyers.'

This time she paled. 'And if you lost your case, I could reciprocate the compliment.'

'You will not win,' he said calmly. 'Believe me. I have always found you most attractive, *cara,* and it would grieve me to see you lose three times what you have already lost. If you proceed with the course of action you've just described, you will probably ruin yourself.'

'Oh, I'm not that poor, either,' she retorted. But he had unnerved her. 'Are you—are you rejecting my offer, then?'

'It's hardly tempting,' he said gently. He leaned forward and took two biscuits from the silver bowl. The dogs sat up alertly. He gave each its titbit, followed by a command which made them both settle obediently under his chair.

Then he looked at her with polite regret and shook his head. 'No, Claudia, I cannot accept your offer. That land belongs to my family, and I'm very much afraid that if you try to take it away from me, I will have no hesitation in prosecuting you to the fullest extent that the law permits.'

It was said so politely, and in such a warm way, that the steel behind the velvet was almost—but not quite—imperceptible.

'That's a great pity,' she said dully. So much for her bright idea! If di Stefano wouldn't take four acres, she knew instinctively that he wouldn't take anything less than the whole. 'In that case, we are going to quarrel, *signore.*'

'There is no quarrel on my side,' he said easily. His

jacket had fallen open slightly, allowing her a glimpse of his taut waist. His shirt was so fine that she could see the curve of hard muscles under the white linen. 'I would much rather make love with you than war. If you have any quarrel, it is with the Rossis. They have taken advantage of you in a most unforgivable way.'

'They were honest!'

'On the contrary, that family have always been most dishonest. Rossi's father was in and out of jail most of his life. Rossi himself is a poacher and a thief, and is no stranger to the inside of Lucca police station.'

'Small crimes, anyway,' she said meaningfully. 'I don't believe that the Rossis have deceived me. I plan to go ahead with occupying my property.' Feeling as tired as a schooner with all the wind knocked out of her sails, Claudia rose to her feet. 'I won't take any more of your time. As they say, see you in court.'

'But you cannot go yet,' he said, raising his eyebrows. That was more emotion than he'd shown through the whole interview, which had left her drained. 'It's been a long time since we last met. Besides, you have seen nothing of the *palazzo*, and there are some remarkable works of art which you really should look at.'

'I'm not in the mood for works of art,' Claudia said joylessly. 'You seem to take all this very lightly, *signore*. Where I come from, matters of this sort are regarded as serious.'

'But of course I take you seriously.' There was a glitter in his eyes for a moment. 'I always have done. However, you must not expect me to treat you like a sworn enemy, just because of this silly incident. That would be too boring.' He rose now, towering over her by at least a foot. 'Shall I tell you the feeling I have always had about you?'

'Surprise me.'

'That if we had more time to spend with one another, a very exciting friendship might be possible between us.'

'Well, we'll never know, will we?' She gave him a look in which anger and unhappiness were combined, and turned to leave. It had been a pointless and depressing afternoon.

And she was going to have to go back and face Vittorio—and Vittorio's family—with nothing to show.

Di Stefano had been toying with her from the start, amusing himself by watching her antics, and no doubt he had thoroughly enjoyed that final, crushing rejection. He walked with her to the hall, lined with towering columns of white marble, interspersed with what were no doubt priceless suits of armour.

'I am sorry to see you so upset——' he began, but Claudia turned on him before he had time to finish the sentence.

'I'm sure you are, *signore*,' she said bitterly. 'But I've had about enough of your mockery for one day.' Her eyes were glittering, cold as emeralds. 'You seem to think I'm a fool, a toy for you to bandy with. You'll find out that I'm not! I can see right through your act, smooth as it is. So no more pleasantries, no more insincere regrets, and *please*, no more sympathy!'

Her voice echoed in the high dome of the hall, bringing an anxious-looking maid to peer from behind a carved oak door.

'You'll wake Great-Aunt Adele,' he said reprovingly, taking her arm as though he didn't notice its stiffness. She tried to pull away, but his fingers were like steel. 'And don't be so prickly. My regret for you is genuine. It is unfortunate that you weren't more circumspect when you bought that property. A good lawyer would have warned you not to touch the deal with a barge pole.'

'The notary——'

'Never buy property without a lawyer. A notary is merely a bureaucrat, not a legal expert. He cannot safeguard you against things like this.' He looked down at her, and it was hard to tell whether his smile was cynical or pitying. 'By all accounts, you know Tuscany well. Surely you know that there are thousands of tenants in the Rossis' position? Can you really see any sane magistrate setting a precedent which would effectively destroy an age-old system of tenantry?' He shook his dark head. 'It's a pipe-dream, Claudia. I know the local judiciary well enough to tell you that you'd be wasting your time. You have been very foolish to base so much money on your own interpretation of the law.'

'I see,' she said thinly. 'In other words, no local magistrate would dare rule against the Duke of Ferraro?'

'That is not what I said.'

'It's what you implied. You're trying to scare me off by saying that the court will be on your side.'

'If you choose to think so,' he shrugged.

'Corruption doesn't scare me either,' she said, her normally soft mouth a tight line. 'You could bribe every judge from here to Rome, but the letter of the law——'

'In Italy,' he said, with more sharpness than he had shown before, 'the letter of the law is very different from the execution of the law.'

She glared at him mutinously. 'Then I will take my case to the International Court of Justice in The Hague,' she snapped.

His eyes narrowed. Without their customary warm smile, they were suddenly as cold as an arctic fiord, and as inimical. 'You are determined to make a fuss, I see,' he said silkily.

'You're damned right I am,' she retorted brusquely. 'The Italian government passed the law, and I bought that property legally and honestly under that law. If a magistrate refuses to uphold the law, I'll take the case to The Hague. I mean it.'

'That might be very unwise,' he said softly.

'Is that a threat?' she asked with a taut expression.

'It's just advice. You're going to lose a lot of sleep, and a lot of money.'

'I have certain rights,' she shot back. 'Why should I let you intimidate me out of them?'

'Your rights?' he repeated with a spark of anger. 'What about my rights, Claudia? It doesn't seem to occur to you that *your* rights involve taking what is mine away from *me!*'

'I offered to split the property with you,' she said pointedly. 'You turned me down. And you have so much land! You'd probably forgotten that farm at Lucca even existed. You can't tell me it will make the slightest difference to your existence!'

'Your logic is superb,' he said with fine sarcasm. 'By the same token, it's better to murder a man named Smith than one named Marjoribanks, because there are so many of them.'

'It's certainly better to steal from the rich than the poor,' Claudia retorted. There was high colour in her cheeks now, and she was breathing faster, as though she'd just been for a brisk walk across the moors. 'Especially the undeserving rich!'

'The undeserving rich?' he repeated, eyes narrowed.

'People like you,' she nodded briskly. 'People born to vast estates which they have neither the interest nor the time to supervise. In this day and age, the concept that one man can grasp at so much land is positively obscene.'

'You have a curious idea of obscenity,' he retorted. 'Are you not, in your turn, trying to grasp at land which belongs to someone else?'

'No, because I bought that land legally, with money which I earned, myself!'

'Your entire moral code seems upside-down to me,' he said with contempt.

'That's because you're standing on your head,' she said with a humourless smile. 'You claim that the Rossis had no right to that land—even though they had lived on it, and worked on it, for generations. Doesn't their sweat give them any rights at all? Did you expect them to remain your serfs, your vassals, your *slaves*, enriching you and your estate for the rest of time?'

'Far from enriching me,' he said bitterly, 'the Rossis have benefited from the generosity of my family for nearly a century, while returning the minimum possible. Had they wanted land of their own, I assure you they have made enough money out of my family to buy an ample tract for their own use. Instead, they chose to have their cake and eat it, too. *You* have just been their dupe, Claudia. Even now, they are laughing themselves sick at your gullibility! As for what I expected from them—I expected them to remain loyal to an agreement which has been well understood in this part of the country for a thousand years.'

'That kind of agreement has been superceded,' she shot back tersely. 'And you, *signore,* stand for a way of life that ought to have been stamped out long ago.'

'Indeed,' he rasped, lowering his head like a bull about to charge. 'Do I contribute so little to the world, then?'

'As far as I can tell,' she said with sparkling eyes,

'what you give to the world is out of all proportion to the wealth and land you have accumulated around you. You do not contribute, *signore*—you exploit.'

'I do not think any further discussion would be helpful,' he said icily. 'Don't let me detain you.'

'The sooner I'm out of this morgue, the better,' she said with deliberate rudeness.

He bowed slightly, and opened one leaf of the huge door for her. Her little car was parked on the gravel outside, and she was suddenly very keen to be in it, and away from this tall, smooth man with the coldly beautiful eyes.

'I have given you good advice,' he told her as she walked down the steps. 'You would be well advised to think over what I have said.'

'And I'm just as serious as you are.' At the bottom of the steps she turned and looked up at him. He looked different from when she'd arrived. The urbane, charming quality had given way to a stillness that almost frightened her. 'Goodbye, *signore*. The next time I see you will probably be in court.'

'I very much doubt whether you will even get as far as the court room.'

The words were said quietly, but with such certainty that she felt a momentary chill crawl across her skin. Twenty generations of breeding had certainly taught him how to convey menace. She shook the chill away, much as she had shaken the chill of twilight Ferraro away a couple of evenings ago.

'Oh, I will,' she assured him. 'Goodbye.'

She got into her car and, without looking back at him or the *palazzo*, drove away.

CHAPTER THREE

NOT exactly a triumph.

In a way, of course, Vito had been right. It was all her own fault, really. Why had she insisted on rushing into such a big purchase without consulting her husband-to-be, or even his family? The whole thing had been something of a *folie de grandeur,* right from the start.

Of course, she hadn't had the slightest idea at that stage that Cesare di Stefano had any claim to the land whatsoever. She might have thought twice before shelling out, if she'd known. Still, it had been an error of judgement to buy that farm so impulsively, no matter how much she'd fallen in love with it.

Maybe she'd just got too rich too quickly. When Colefax & Brennan had really taken off, two years ago, she'd turned almost overnight from a struggling businessperson with a nose for good wine, into a surprisingly wealthy young lady. She'd found herself with the capital and income to live the kind of life she'd always dreamed of.

Yet she'd been frugal. Her frugality, according to Vittorio, was her saving grace.

She'd resisted the Porsche, she'd resisted the fur coat, she'd even resisted travelling first-class on aeroplanes. But she hadn't been able to resist seventeen acres of terraced vineyards overlooking Lucca.

Buying that vineyard had been her first real extravagance. And it looked as though it was going to prove even more extravagant than she'd bargained for. Determined as she was to fight di Stefano for it, she had no illusions that it would prove a long and expensive battle.

These reflections, passing through her mind as she drove back to meet Vito in Pisa, put her in a mind-softened mood towards him. She'd been over-confident and brash, and she was quite prepared to admit the error of her ways.

It was unfortunate that Vito's reaction happened to be one calculated to set her teeth on edge.

He laughed bitterly. 'I told you so.'

'Yes,' she agreed sourly, 'you told me so.'

'So, apart from alienating the man, and threatening him with the International Court of Justice, what did you achieve?'

'Nothing.'

'Exactly, nothing. Except that by angering your opponent, you have made him all the more dangerous.'

'I'm pretty angry myself,' she gritted.

'You should never have gone to him in the first place. Now that you have provoked him, he may take pre-emptive action.'

She gave him a dry look. 'Should I be on the look-out for the assassin's dagger, then?'

'I think you can expect an injunction, at any rate,' he declared. 'And if, as you say, he is talking about re-letting the property, you've practically lost already. With sitting tenants in the farm again, possessed of a legal contract with di Stefano, you don't have a hope in hell of getting that property back.' Vito signalled for two more drinks. They were sitting in the plush bar of her hotel in Pisa. Claudia, trying to unwind over a glass or two of wine, found her attitude towards Vito hardening rapidly. His response, of course, was very predictable, but none the less annoying for that. 'Not that you had a hope in hell to start with,' he concluded.

'I don't care,' she said shortly. 'I meant what I said to him. I fully intend to take this to The Hague.'

'Claudia, for God's sake!'

'It's my right,' she snapped, repeating what she'd said to Cesare di Stefano. 'If the government won't uphold my right, then I shall appeal to a higher authority.'

'You'll spend the rest of your life embroiled in this case,' Vito said in a hard voice. 'And for what? For a ramshackle old farm and a few acres of neglected grapes?' He paid the barman, and turned back to her. 'We must attack the Rossis, Claudia, and attack them now!'

'Why should they give up the money?' she demanded. 'What will they do if they have to give the money back? Then they'll have no home to go to, and no money to buy another!'

'That's their problem. You're too sentimental, Claudia. No matter how clever they are,' Vito went on with evident satisfaction, 'women should never, *ever*, get involved in buying property without a man's advice.'

'Well, as it happens, this one has,' she said acidly.

'And look how it's turned out! I hope you'll stay well out of it from now on,' he said meaningfully. 'This is not the kind of problem, my dear, that a woman on her own can solve.'

She made an explosive noise. 'Just what has my being a woman got to do with it, anyway?' she said irritably. 'This could have happened to anyone, male or female. I'm just as good as any man, Vito. I've proved that.'

Vito's expression was infuriatingly complacent. 'You think so?'

'Yes, I do. I don't see that any of this has anything to do with my sex!'

'In England, maybe not. In Italy, your sex has a lot to do with it. It marks you out as vulnerable. A target, in other words. The Rossis saw you coming a mile off, and they've taken you for a ride. A big one.' He smacked his lips over the wine. 'Which is exactly why you need a man's protection. Every Italian woman knows that.'

'Oh, I'm certain,' she said shortly, reaching for her own drink, 'that an Italian woman would have handled things far better.'

'Italian women don't behave the way you do,' he said with a touch of bitterness. 'That's how they stay out of this sort of trouble. An Italian woman wouldn't have dreamed of buying property without her man's approval.'

'Yes, Vito, I know. Italian women defer to the all-wise, all-powerful Italian male in every department of life.'

'They let themselves be guided by their husbands,' he said significantly.

'You're not my husband *yet*,' she pointed out, equally significantly. 'And I'm not going to be meek and deferential because of my sex, Vito. Not to you or anyone else. So you might as well learn to live with it!'

'I don't like you to speak to me like that,' he said,

eyebrows coming down darkly.

'And I don't care to be patronised,' she snapped. She gulped down the wine with unusual—and unwise—speed. 'You forget that I bought that house so we could get married!'

'You gambled a great deal of money that should have stayed in the bank,' he said pointedly. His mouth was handsome, but had a tendency towards sternness, which was coming out now. 'Money that would have been very useful to us right now. As it happens, there is a very suitable property which I had my eye on, near San Gemigniano. I was thinking of making an offer for it this month.'

'Well, as it happens, you should have told me sooner.'

'It did not concern you.'

'Oh, didn't it? You were going to buy a house for us to live in without my even seeing it?'

'That's exactly what you did,' he retorted.

Her eyes flashed. 'The difference being that I'm the one who is expected to pay for the place.'

He looked at her from under lowered brows. 'That's insulting. But it does not change the argument. You are living proof of the fickleness of women, Claudia—clever enough to make a fortune one day, stupid enough to throw it all away the next.'

Claudia stared at him, speechless. Then she picked up her handbag. 'Keep talking like that, Vittorio,' she advised him angrily, 'and you might never have to put up with marriage to me at *all*.'

She stalked out of the bar, and was not surprised when Vito didn't follow.

Though they made it up to some extent on Saturday

morning, Claudia and Vito were barely on speaking terms over the rest of the weekend; and though she went ahead with her business as usual, making the rounds of the local wine-farmers, she was conscious of feeling lost. Not just because of her quarrel with Vito, which had been sharper and more unpleasant than most; she was also lost about what to do as regarded the farm at Lucca.

Her show of bravado towards Cesare di Stefano had run out of steam. Just how *did* one go about appealing to the International Court of Justice? Obviously, you couldn't do that until you had failed to receive justice through the usual channels. And that meant she would still have to face an Italian lawsuit, with all its attendant expenses and complications. As Vito had cheerfully pointed out, it might be years before she got to the stage of even having a case to present to the Court of Justice. And by then, she might already have spent more in legal fees than the farm was worth.

Did she really have the stamina to go through with all that? Would it not be simpler, as Vito had advised, to try and get the money back from the Rossis?

The trouble was a question of principle. She believed that the Rossis had sold in good faith, and she really didn't feel she had the right to try and take the money back again, effectively leaving them both penniless and homeless. And that was assuming she won her case against them, which she very much doubted was likely.

So where did that leave her? Still in conflict with Cesare di Stefano. But was she going to try and take possession of the farm, and face a prosecution for trespass? Or was she going to go on the attack by taking out a suit against him? Who was going to be suing whom?

She was no further forward in her thinking by Sunday afternoon, when she drove out to the Zanoletti estate.

Vini Zanoletti SpA was a medium-sized estate, but a prestigious one. It produced a *Chianti classico* of great flavour and distinction, which had been well received by her more discriminating clients over the past couple of years.

Ugo Zanoletti himself was out in the vineyards when she arrived, working with his three sons. Unlike some wine-producers of the area, he left none of the important jobs to workers, preferring to do them himself, or at least have them done under his own eye.

She walked through the fields of leafy vines, their canopies higher than a man's head, to meet him. It was hot, and the fruit was already starting to give off a grapy smell in the dusty air. The baking hills all around were turning brown and parched, only the olives and cypresses looking fresh.

She was braless under her pretty white frock, and wearing a wide-brimmed straw hat, but she was fiercely hot, none the less, and wishing, as she always did in summer, that parasols were still in fashion.

Zanoletti, a burly, grizzled man in his seventies, barely paused in his work to greet her, but she was not put off by his brusqueness. She got on well with him, and respected him as a man with a vast knowledge of everything connected with wine.

She nodded a greeting to his sons, all working shirt-less in the heat, and fanned herself with her straw hat.

'Nice weather.'

'If it holds. Another six hundred cases this year?' Zanoletti asked, cropping at the glowing bunches of grapes with his pruning shears.

'I think I can sell a thousand, Don Ugo,' Claudia said. 'If the price is right, of course.'

'With wine, you only get what you pay for,' he grunted. 'You know that, Claudia. But don't worry. The price will be right. Bear with me while I prune this row, then we can talk business—over a glass.'

'I didn't mean to interrupt you.'

'I'm ready for a pause, anyway. I'm getting too old for this work. I'll let my boys finish off the job. Besides,' he smiled, 'it's no hardship to take a glass of wine with a beautiful woman on a Sunday afternoon.'

'I didn't realise you pruned the vines at this time of the year,' she remarked, watching as the immature clusters of grapes fell to the ground under the rough but expert pruning.

He squinted at her, his mahogany-tanned face a maze of wrinkles. 'Not everybody does it. But we've always done it. We cut out all the primary growth,' he said, showing her by action. 'I only want bunches from the main stock.'

'But why?' she asked, keeping pace with him as he moved along the row. 'You'll only get a third of the amount of wine. Other farmers are happy to have as many grapes as they can get on each vine!'

'Other farmers produce *vinello*,' he growled in scorn. 'Thin, cheap wine that has no distinction. You can only get good wine out of good grapes, Claudia. See how I cut away all this growth?' The shears hacked apparently aimlessly at the vine, but the cuts were accurate and swift. 'That leaves the principal bunches of fruit to develop fully. The grapes will be fewer—but they will also be bigger, sweeter, juicier. Look.' He showed her how he cropped away the overhanging canopy of leaves as well. 'This is also important. This lets the sun get to the grapes that are left. The action of sunlight on the skin of the fruit makes it ripen properly. That way you get all the flavour, all the special substances that make a truly good wine. Then it will ferment better, mature better, and keep longer. And you know, it's the skin of the grape that gives a wine the true bouquet. Otherwise all you are making is fermented fruit juice.'

'I'm learning all your secrets,' she smiled, storing away this piece of lore in her mind. 'No wonder your wines are the best in the region.'

'I'm not afraid of the competition. Others are too greedy to do what I do—they'd rather sell three times the quantity of poor wine.'

'You should put it all in a book, Don Ugo.'

'Me? I can hardly write my name. But I'll make a deal with you—*you* write the book, and I'll give you all the information to put in it.'

'That's not a bad idea,' she said thoughtfully, watching Zanoletti's deft, experienced movements. Despite the heat, he didn't seem to be sweating a drop, as unaffected by the sun as a gnarled old oak tree. There was probably more real knowledge in that grizzled head than in most encyclopaedias about wine. The germ of an idea dawned in her mind. 'Not a bad idea at all.'

The farmer snapped off a last tendril, and pocketed his shears with a sigh. 'That's enough for one afternoon. Let's go up and sit in the *portico*.'

The shady *portico* of the old farmhouse doubled as veranda and drying-room. A huge refectory table, set out on the stone-flagged floor, always bore wine and fruit for visitors to the estate, while up in the cool darkness above hams and other produce of the farm—salamis and various other sausages, great strings of onions and garlic, peppers, tomatoes and bunches of herbs—hung from the rafters to cure and dry.

Zanoletti excused himself to go and wash. While Claudia sat waiting, one of his daughters smilingly prepared the table: a large *fiasco* of Chianti in its traditional straw cradle, a basket of crusty farm bread, and a plate piled with delicious, wafer-thin slices of Parma ham.

When the old farmer returned, in a clean white shirt, there was a gleam in his eye. He sat down, poured three glasses of wine, as though he were expecting another guest, and squinted at her brightly. 'I hear you are in the wars, young lady.'

She gave him a careful glance from under the brim of her hat. 'Why do you say that?'

'A little bird tells me you are clashing horns with a certain titled gentleman of these parts.'

'Huh!' Claudia snorted. 'Nothing is private in Tuscany, it seems!'

'Word gets around. *Salute.*'

'*Salute.*' She took a mouthful of the delicious wine, and murmured a compliment about the vintage.

Zanoletti smacked his lips approvingly. 'Not bad. A thousand cases, you say?'

'If the price is right,' she repeated casually. After a decent interval of conversation, she knew, they would get down to the haggling Zanoletti so enjoyed, and would eventually arrive at a price that suited them both.

Zanoletti admired the ruby tint of his own product. 'So it's true about you and di Stefano, then?' he asked.

'Let's say there is a dispute about some land,' she admitted cautiously.

Ugo Zanoletti grunted, and passed her the ham.

'I know the property in question. It's a nice place. But you've taken on the wrong one there, Claudia. He gives the impression of being easy-going, like a cat sleeping in a creamery. But you will find he is a tiger when he wakes. And he is as hard as a stone beneath the smile.'

'I think I'm beginning to realise that,' she said wryly. 'But I don't have much choice, Don Ugo. I stand to lose a lot of money if I just give in.'

'The Rossis have cheated you. Go after them, not di Stefano.'

'But that land was theirs!'

'That land is his,' Zanoletti said in his brusque way, concentrating on pouring two more glassfuls. 'It has been in his family for centuries. Everyone knows that.'

Claudia took her hat off, and laid it on the floor beside her. 'You think di Stefano is in the right, then? You're on his side?'

'I did not say that. But why should a man's lands be taken away from him? There is no justice in that.'

Claudia sighed. 'There *is* justice in it. Laws have been passed recently——'

'I know all about those laws,' the old man cut in contemptuously. 'Bad laws, designed to cause trouble between landlord and tenant. How can an estate like the di Stefanos' survive, if such laws are put into practice?'

'Maybe estates like the di Stefanos' aren't *meant* to survive,' Claudia said pointedly.

'Oh? And what does that mean?'

'Their day has passed. I think it's shocking that so much wealth should be allowed to stay in one man's hands!'

'Do you?' Zanoletti looked as though he were

enjoying some private joke. 'I had no idea you were such an anarchist, Claudia.'

'I'm not an anarchist, and you know it,' she retorted. 'I believe in democracy and equality, though, and Italy could always do with a little more democracy and equality,' she said meaningfully. 'Sometimes it's positively feudal. Di Stefano did not create the wealth to buy that land, did he? He never had to work for it?'

'No,' the old man agreed, 'it was left to him by his father.'

'Exactly. Whereas the Rossis broke their backs to cultivate the farm for three generations!'

Ugo made a noise like a rusty gate closing. 'No Rossi ever broke his back working at anything.'

Claudia ignored that remark. 'Why should one man own half the province, just because of his name? Why should he possess such vast wealth, unearned?'

Something like a smile stretched Zanoletti's mouth. 'Good questions. You'll be able to ask him those things yourself in a short while.'

'What do you mean?' she asked warily.

'I'm expecting Cesare di Stefano at three,' he told her, consulting his battered pocket watch. 'Any minute, in fact. He's coming to look at a horse of mine he's thinking of buying.' His eyes gleamed at her expression of discomfort. 'We can all enjoy a glass of wine together. And you can tell him your opinion of the feudal system.'

That explained the third glass of wine. The news was scarcely welcome. Claudia felt her heart sinking as she took another sip of wine. But there wasn't much she could do, short of scuttling off in undignified haste, her business with Zanoletti unconcluded, and that was unthinkable. She would have to stay and confront di Stefano. But it was bad luck.

And the rumble of a powerful engine informed her that she wouldn't have very long to wait.

'Here he is now,' Zanoletti said with satisfaction.

A low-slung red sports car—a Ferrari, naturally —nosed into the farmyard, scattering chickens. With a muted roar, it halted next to Claudia's own little Fiat. The door opened, and Cesare di Stefano swung himself out.

Claudia and Ugo Zanoletti had risen to meet him, she with a set and expressionless face, he with a craggy grin.

Di Stefano, however, was not smiling his usual catlike smile as he came up the stairs to meet them. His manners, though, were as immaculate as ever. 'Ah,' he said, towering over them both, 'I see I've arrived in time for a glass of excellent Zanoletti wine. What a delicious surprise to see you here, Claudia.' His eyes drifted over her figure, assessingly but without warmth. 'You look as fresh as a lily in this heat. And how are you, Don Ugo?'

'As well as an old man can expect to be, *signore.*' He ushered di Stefano to the vacant chair, and went on with more than a touch of devilment, 'Claudia and I were discussing the land laws of Italy. Oddly enough, your name cropped up in the course of the discussion.'

'Ah, yes?' The grey eyes gave Claudia a cool glance. 'And why was that?'

'Claudia is one of those who feel that the great estates of the past should be broken up,' Zanoletti said innocently, and raised his glass. 'Your health, *signore.*'

Cesare di Stefano did not touch his glass. 'Yes,' he said drily, 'I am aware of Claudia's views on the great estates of the past.'

'She also wondered,' Zanoletti went on with relish, 'why a single man should be allowed to own so much wealth when he had neither sweated for it, nor paid for it out of his own pocket, simply inherited it from his family.'

Claudia opened her mouth in dismay. 'I didn't mean——'

'Perhaps,' di Stefano said icily, cutting through her stammering defence, 'Claudia is not as well informed as she thinks she is. I pay for the land I own, every day of my life.'

'I was talking in a general sense,' Claudia said fretfully, cursing the old man for his malicious sense of humour. 'I wasn't referring to anyone in particular.'

'That is all the more reason,' di Stefano retorted coldly, 'why you should seek to disguise your own ignorance, and not air it in public.'

'I'm not so ignorant that I cannot see the truth, *signore,*' Claudia said, stung by the rebuke. 'But I don't want to argue with you here. We're both guests of Don Ugo.'

'Please! I enjoy a vigorous discussion,' the old man said with another rusty laugh. On his weathered face was an expression Claudia had seen on the faces of boys at a dog-fight. 'In any case, the girl has a point. How *do* you justify inherited wealth, *signore?*'

'I don't have to justify it,' he replied forcefully, drumming his fingertips irritably on the table. 'Being able to leave one's property to one's children is a fundamental human right. What else does a man work for?' The glittering grey eyes fixed on Claudia. 'All your immature babbling about wealth and aristocracy is just a cover for your own cupidity. You look for a noble philosophy to cover the fact of your own theft,' he added in a harsher tone.

'Theft?'

'What else is it?' he shrugged. 'The Rossis have stolen from you. You now seek to steal from me. Your greed is understandable, of course,' he said with a cold smile. 'But your moralising is rather tedious.'

Pale with anger, Claudia rose to her feet. 'I will not stay here to be insulted by you,' she said in a shaky voice. She turned to Don Ugo, who was looking as though he distinctly regretted having stirred up this hornet's nest. 'Please excuse me, Don Ugo. We will have to discuss those thousand cases on some other occasion.'

The two men rose to their feet. The old farmer was looking extremely uncomfortable, but on the face of Cesare di Stefano there was only a cold contempt.

'I should never have raised the subject,' the old man muttered. 'It was an ill choice.'

'The subject would have arisen of its own accord,' di Stefano said indifferently. He turned to Claudia. 'I will walk you to your car.'

Leaving Don Ugo mourning over the bottle of wine, Cesare di Stefano escorted Claudia in silence to her little Fiat.

He opened the door for her. Before she got in, she turned to him, and looked tensely up into the hard-eyed face. 'To call me a thief, *signore*, was not only ungallant and untrue; it was unmanly.'

'To imply that I am a parasite was hardly lady-like, either,' he retorted drily. The handsome face held no gentleness or repentance. 'From your attitude this afternoon, I take it you are still bent on your plan of contesting the ownership of the farm with me?'

'More than ever,' she said fiercely. 'It's rapidly becoming a point of principle, in fact! If you were so keen to hang on to that land,' she went on, her eyes sparkling with anger, 'then you should have looked after it a damned sight better. The house is falling to pieces, the olives are unpicked, and the vineyard is deteriorating, while you sit in your gilded *palazzo* among all your possessions and entertain Great-Aunt Adele. That's exactly the kind of decadence those land laws were passed to remedy. If you won't care for the land, then you should let it pass to someone who will.'

'Who let the land decay?' he said in contempt. 'I or the Rossis? They are the decadent parasites, not me. And what foolish idealist made the law that prevented me from doing anything about it? Someone, my dear Claudia, not unlike yourself!'

'Well, thank God there are more people who think like me than there are who think like you!' She compressed her lips. 'You are an anachronism, Your Excellency. People like you, born to own vast tracts of land that they can't even supervise, ought to be as dead as the dinosaurs!'

'Thank you,' he said ironically. Odd how grim those good looks became when he wasn't doing his Cheshire-cat routine! The shadows over his eyes and under his cheekbones made him suddenly almost sinister. 'Except that I am most definitely alive, and kicking. Take my advice. Forget that farm. Get your money back from the Rossis, and be more careful next time.'

'That farm is mine!' She said it with venom.

His eyes narrowed. 'I have warned you once before, Claudia. You do not have the resources to oppose me. You will bitterly regret having taken this path.'

'Are you trying to threaten me?' she asked sharply.

'I am trying to warn you,' he said silkily. His eyes were arctic. 'Be warned. For your own sake.'

'Insults—and now intimidation,' she sneered. 'You're a fine example of Tuscan nobility, *signore*.' She got behind the wheel, slammed the door, and started the engine. Before putting the Fiat into gear, she wound down the window, and looked up at him. 'Here's a warning for you, Your Excellency,' she said crisply. 'I intend to fight you for that farm. And I intend to win.'

Without waiting for a reply, she reversed backwards, swung through a gaggle of clucking chickens, and headed towards the road, leaving him a dark, forbidding figure in her rear-view mirror.

On Tuesday afternoon, Claudia decided to go back to Zanoletti, both to confirm that order for a thousand cases of Chianti, and to apologise for losing her temper. Not that Zanoletti had been exactly diplomatic that afternoon, but, now that her temper had had a day or two to cool off, she regretted having made such a display of herself in front of the old man.

About di Stefano, on the other hand, she didn't give a damn. In fact, she still derived an inner satisfaction from having given him a piece of her mind in such a blunt way. No doubt it had been a novel experience for the Duke of Ferraro, especially coming from a woman. Well, high time Cesare di Stefano realised that he was living in the twentieth century, and not in the sixteenth!

She set off around three, after having stopped off in Ferraro to speak to Vito. Relations with her fiancé were still rather sensitive, and her mind was troubled as she drove through the remote countryside towards the Zanoletti estate.

She'd noticed the big grey truck in her rear-view mirror for some time. It had appeared soon after she'd left the outskirts of Ferraro, but it had seemed to hang back for several kilometres. It wasn't until she got on to the long, lonely stretch of road that crossed the hills that it moved up close behind her.

It was now so close that all she could see in her mirror was the grille, and the roar of its diesel had drowned out the quieter note of her own engine.

Italian truck-drivers were the bane of her life. They could be so arrogant, so careless of life. It frightened her to have this great beast roaring and snorting down her neck. The road was quite empty, and in the deep afternoon shadow, the Tuscan hills had taken on a savage, eerie atmosphere. There was nowhere on the narrow road to pull over, so she accelerated instead.

They were going downhill now, and the big grey truck had no difficulty in keeping up with her. She started in alarm as its klaxon sounded an imperious yodel from behind her. If anything, he was closer than before, the grinning teeth of his grille practically snapping at her rear. What the hell did he expect her to do? Crawl into the undergrowth to let him by?

He was so close that she dared not slow down or swerve. All she could do was keep speeding on, with her heart in her mouth.

The road widened slightly as it levelled out on to the plain, and she pulled over to the right to let him get by. With a crash of shifting gears, he swung out alongside her and started to overtake.

It seemed to take him ages. The great grey truck crept by her, taking up almost the entire road, the fumes of its diesel billowing all around her. She read the sign on the side of the cab: 'VINI DI STEFANO'. One of the noble Duke's trucks, she realised with a flash of anger. This driver had no doubt learned his manners from his master!

One set of Claudia's wheels were in the gutter, bumping uncomfortably over the ruts, and she cursed impatiently. He'd been so keen to get past; if he didn't hurry up and get it over with, another car would come along in the opposite direction and they'd all be killed.

Suddenly, she saw the bridge. A narrow stone bridge, coming up fast. And the di Stefano truck was deliberately squeezing her off the road!

There was no time to do anything but swerve violently to avoid hitting the stone pillar. She stamped hard on the brakes, but the wheels were skidding helplessly on grass now. The little car slithered over the edge of the bank, and to her horror, Claudia realised that, far from a shallow stream, a deep chasm yawned below her.

For a split-second the car was poised over the abyss. In that moment of sheer terror, she had time to curl up defensively and protect her head with her arms.

She was being murdered. Murdered on the orders of a man with ice-cold grey eyes.

And then she was toppling fast into the shadowy depths.

CHAPTER FOUR

CLAUDIA was staring dreamily at a beautiful field of flowers. The flowers were all colours, but the colours were pleasingly muted, almost faded. There were animals, too. A dappled doe browsed among the primroses, while the stag watched a distant hunting party without alarm. A cherry-tree nearby was almost as full of partridges as it was of flowers. A hare leaped with springtime energy over a bush that was starry with blossoms. Everywhere was life and sweetness.

It was a lovely scene.

The odd thing was that it was all above her. She was lying on her back, staring *up* at this field. That puzzled her for a long time, but it didn't make the scene any the less charming, or the colours any the less pleasing.

Finally, the scene moved. Gentle hands lifted her, propping her up against pillows, the way she'd propped her dolls up as a girl. With doll-like surprise she registered that the scene was an embroidered canopy above her, and that she had been lying in a huge four-poster bed. At the corners of the bed were four golden angels. The bed itself was in a beautiful, feminine room whose windows looked out on to a sunlit park not unlike the one in the embroidery.

But the bed, the room, and the two women who were propping her up in bed, were utterly strange to her.

'What has happened' she asked, dry-mouthed with long sleep. 'Where am I?'

Just relax, *signorina*. You are quite well.'

64

The answer had come in Italian, and it was as though that had unplugged her bottled-up memory.

Images came rushing back. The truck. The bridge. Falling into the black chasm of that riverbed.

Claudia struggled upright in alarm. 'He tried to kill me,' she said breathlessly. 'I must speak to the police!'

'Calma, signorina, calma.' She'd cried out in English, and they hadn't understood. They were trying to soothe her as though she were a fretful child. *'Non si recorda di niente?'*

'No,' she replied, looking at them with big eyes that were pale green with fear. 'I don't remember anything. Please tell me what has happened to me!'

'You were brought here last night,' the older of the two maids informed her. She reached for a silver-backed brush, and started brushing Claudia's rich red hair with gentle, expert strokes.

'Such beautiful hair, *signorina,*' the other sighed enviously, fastening the chemise at her throat. Under the silky garment she was naked. She had been undressed and put into this strange bed like a helpless little girl. Where was Vittorio? Why wasn't he here?

'Who are you?' she asked numbly.

'My name is Anna. You were very lucky not to have been badly hurt, *signorina.*' She turned Claudia's arm over, and showed her the big purple bruise on her forearm. As though it hadn't existed until now, it started to throb dully, and she became aware of other bruises, other pains starting up all over her body. There were several cuts on her hands, which also hurt, but none of them had been bad enough to need bandaging. She recognised the pink stains of mercurochrome. She stared at herself, remembering that horrible plunge. God, she'd been lucky!

'You were covered in broken glass,' Anna went on.

'It took us an hour to get it all out of your hair. But for the safety-belt, it would have been much, much worse. You hardly seemed to know where you were. The doctor said you were badly shocked——'

'The doctor?' Claudia interrupted, looking up from her poor hands. 'What doctor?'

'Dottore Ortolani. His Excellency's personal physician.' Anna swept the gleaming swathes back from Claudia's pale face, and smiled at her reassuringly. 'He gave you a sleeping draught, and left orders that you were to stay in bed for at least forty-eight hours. Your car, I'm afraid, is finished. They are going to try and pull it out of the river later today.'

She stared at the pleasant country face in silence. Her heart was pounding. She knew where she was, now. In the house of the man who had tried to kill her.

'I want to see my fiancé,' she said urgently. 'Where is he?'

'Your fiancé?' Anna nodded. 'Ah, yes—you mean Signor Brunelli? He came to see you last night, and again this morning, but you were asleep both times. The doctor gave strict orders that you were not to be disturbed on any account, *signorina.*'

Poor Vito must be as worried as hell about her, she realised. 'I must use the telephone,' she said, looking from one to the other.

'You should rest, *signorina.*' It was a polite but firm refusal. 'Your hotel has been informed,' Anna went on. 'They are sending some clothes and toiletries over this morning.'

'But I'm not staying!' Claudia protested, wide-eyed.

'The doctor was quite specific——'

'I must get back to my fiancé, my work! I've got appointments, people to meet, all sorts of things to do!

There's nothing wrong with me!'

'Your nervous system has had a shock.' The tone was kindly, but uncompromising. 'You must remain in bed until tomorrow at least, and even after that, you should continue to rest.'

'I don't feel ill.' Claudia's mouth had set in a mutinous line. To stay here, in the house of a man who had probably tried to bump her off, was intolerable. 'I'd like my clothes, please.'

'They are being laundered,' Anna said apologetically. 'Everything was filthy, and there was some blood, too.'

'Damn!' Claudia said ungratefully. She gnawed her lip. 'What has happened to the truck driver, anyway?' she asked.

'Happened?'

'He nearly killed me,' she snapped. 'He ought to be in custody.'

Shock clouded Anna's face. 'Oh, I'm sure you must be mistaken, *signorina*. I know the man, and he is a good driver. It was he who brought you back here, and he was most upset.'

'I'll bet he was. So he's walking around free?' she asked acidly.

'Well, *driving* around,' the maid corrected with the ghost of a smile. 'He is on his way to Switzerland now, with a consignment of the master's wines. It was just an accident, *signorina*.'

'What about the police?'

'The police have been informed. But since there was no collision, and only one car involved, they are not making any enquiries.'

Claudia stared at her bitterly. So that was the way they were going to play it. One of Cesare di Stefano's lorries deliberately tried to kill one of Cesare di

Stefano's enemies, and it was just an accident. *You will bitterly regret having taken this path.* That was what he had said. *I very much doubt whether you will even get as far as the court room.* He'd said that, too. And he'd meant it.

She caught the glance that passed between the two servants. To them, her suspicion was probably evidence of delayed shock. They didn't know.

'What time is it?' she demanded.

'Almost ten,' Anna smiled. 'Would you like some breakfast?'

'Just coffee.'

'No coffee—on the *dottore's* orders. How about hot chocolate?'

Claudia made a face. 'I hate hot chocolate.' She plucked at the chemise. 'Isn't there *anything* I can wear apart from this?'

'But of course.' A light silk dressing-gown appeared from out of a cupboard, and the two women helped her on with it. It was exquisitely embroidered, and the luxurious feel of it did a lot to help ease her tension.

'A lady to the manner born.'

The deep male voice came from the doorway. Claudia's eyes widened as she met Cesare di Stefano's ironic gaze. He walked into the room, one hand in his pocket. 'I've been listening to you bullying my staff,' he remarked drily. 'I'm glad you're not an aristocrat, Claudia. You would give the rest of us a bad name.'

'You—you tried to kill me,' she whispered.

He stared down at her for a moment, then laughed with contempt. 'My dear girl! Had I tried to kill you, I assure you that you would now be conducting this conversation via a medium.'

Her slender fingers were at her throat, as though his very presence threatened her. 'You wanted me out of the way,' she said, staring at him with big, frightened eyes. 'You sent that truck——'

'But you're not out of the way,' he pointed out drily. 'You're still here. And a truck? So messy. I would have thought up something far more elegant, so as not to spoil your beauty. A few drops of deadly nightshade in your Chianti, perhaps.' He nodded to the two maids, who melted away obediently, leaving them alone together. 'In any case,' he went on, sitting on the bed beside her, 'whatever method I chose, you would certainly not have woken up again.' He turned her arm over to study the bruise. His fingers were warm on her skin, and she flinched at his touch. 'See? You were very lucky.'

'Your truck driver ought to be in jail.' Far from convinced by his retorts, she looked at him with mingled dislike and fear. 'If you didn't pay him to run me off the road, then he's a pig of a driver!'

'Giuseppe is no worse than most, and better than many.' He was studying her hand now, examining her fingers as though handling some delicate but inanimate work of art. 'From what he told me, the fault was mainly yours.'

She snatched her hand away. *'Mine?'*

'You should have slowed down to let him over-take, especially on a narrow road. That's basic road sense. Trying to race a man who's overtaking you in a twenty-ton lorry is hardly sensible.'

She glowered at him. He was wearing a white silk polo-neck, which brought out the full drama of his good looks. The fine material clung to the muscles of his chest and arms, presenting a very different image from yesterday's formal elegance. In the casual clothes, his presence disturbed her—and not just because she was more than half-afraid of him. His face was so distinctive that it took some time to realise just how incredibly handsome he was. When he smiled into her eyes, the way he was doing now, there was a curious hollow feeling inside her. 'Why wasn't I taken to a hospital, anyway?' she demanded ungraciously.

He shrugged. 'The *palazzo* was closer. My doctor saw you immediately, and assured me that no hospitalisation was necessary, only full rest. I've taken the liberty of dealing with the local *carabinieri*, and Hertz, myself—I'm sure you don't want to be bothered with all that.'

'Well, I can't stay here!'

'Where else do you intend to go?'

'Back to my hotel, of course,' she retorted.

'Completely out of the question,' he said authoritatively. 'You must stay here until you are well enough to be moved.'

'But I don't *want* to stay here,' she protested in frustration.

'I don't particularly *want* to have you,' he retorted coolly. 'Especially not when you behave so poorly. It's a great pity,' he said in a velvety voice, 'that your upbringing does not match your considerable beauty. Though it is ungallant to say so, I had not realised until yesterday quite how beautiful you are. It was not until I undressed you last night that I——'

'You undressed me?' she exclaimed, sitting up in shock.

'*Carissima*—you have nothing at all to be ashamed of.' His heavy-lidded eyes were mocking. 'I'd always wondered what lay beneath those determinedly English clothes. The reality exceeded my most hopeful dreams. A body like yours is one of nature's masterpieces.'

'How dared you!' She snatched her hand away. The scarlet in her cheeks was from anger now, not embarrassment.

Pointless though the gesture was, she pulled the sheets up to her chin. The thought of those mocking grey eyes studying her unconscious nakedness sent hot and cold flushes all over her skin.

His smile was pure wickedness. 'How refreshing to see the confident Miss Brennan reduced to blushes,' he said pleasantly. 'Tell me, how did you come by that scar on your thigh? Such an intimate place. I wondered . . .'

She didn't let him finish. This time she pulled the sheets right over her head and squeezed her eyes shut, senselessly willing the earth to swallow her, scar and all.

Strong fingers pulled the sheet away. 'Don't be such a goose,' he said brusquely.

'You're hateful,' she gritted, still burning hot inside and out.

'That serves you right for calling me a murderer, then,' he retorted. 'I've never heard such impudence.'

She met his eyes with difficulty. She'd never, ever be able to face him without embarrassment again. 'If you could do *that,*' she accused thickly, 'how do you expect me to believe you had nothing to do with the accident?'

'Oh, come!' he snorted. 'You talk like an impressionable girl. Of course I had nothing to do with it. Do you really think I would try and kill you over a few worthless vines?'

'They weren't so worthless on Sunday,' she said, sitting up more combatively. 'You made threats against my life on Sunday!'

'Claudia, be rational!'

'From what I hear of your family,' she said, plucking at the sheet with restless fingers, 'a murder or two isn't exactly unusual.'

'I assure you,' he drawled, 'it has been at least a

century since any member of my family murdered anyone. And, apart from a cardinal who poisoned two of his mistresses in 1509, the di Stefanos *never* kill women.'

Something in the mocking tone rebuked Claudia, and she dropped her eyes. She smoothed the sheet where she had plucked it. 'Well,' she said mutinously, 'you can't deny that it looks extremely suspicious.'

'Oh, no doubt,' he said ironically. 'Highly suspicious.' He rose, and looked down at her. 'Try and get some rest now. The doctor will be here to see you later this evening. And give that fevered imagination of yours a rest.'

She shrugged sullenly in answer, and he left the room, closing the door behind him.

As soon as she was alone, she sat up in bed, and turned her attention to the bedside table. In the space under the top drawer, she found what she wanted. A telephone. Purposefully, she lifted it out, checked that it was plugged in, and punched Vittorio's number into the handset.

His voice lifted in mingled anxiety and relief. 'Claudia! Thank God. How do you feel? Are you all right?'

'I've been worse.' She switched to English, which Vittorio spoke perfectly well, just in case anyone was eavesdropping. 'Listen, they won't let me out of here. I need you!'

'What do you mean, they won't let you out?' he said, sounding worried. 'Are you hurt, or something?'

'I'm just bruised. There's really nothing else wrong with me. I keep trying to tell them, but they won't listen. And they say my clothes are all being washed. Listen to me. The hotel is sending some of my clothes over this morning. As soon as I've got them, I'll be ready to go. Can you come over with a car and pick me up?'

'Yes, of course,' Vito said. 'If you're absolutely sure you're all right, that is?'

'I'm just shaken. I'll be fine once I'm back in my own bed.'

'How did you manage to pick a di Stefano truck, by the way, out of all the trucks in Tuscany?' Now that his relief at hearing her voice was subsiding, a note of acid had crept into her fiancé's tone. 'This is turning into a farce, Claudia.'

'A farce?' she echoed drily. 'What makes you think it was an accident?'

'What do you mean?'

'You said yourself that di Stefano is a dangerous man,' she said meaningfully.

There was a pause. 'You're joking,' he scoffed.

'I am not,' she said sharply. 'It was deliberate, Vittorio. He says it wasn't, but I don't believe him. I'll tell you exactly what happened when you get here.'

'I'll be there as soon as I can get away from work,' he said briskly. 'Anything else?'

'Just get here.'

Claudia was feeling slightly better as she replaced the handset, and put the phone back under the drawer. Step one accomplished. Step two was to get into the bathroom that led off the bedroom she was in. If she was going to leave here this morning, she'd better practise getting out of bed right now.

Gingerly, she emerged from the covers, and got to her feet. It was a mistake. After a few steps, a wave of giddiness washed over her, and she only just reached the bathroom without toppling over. Leaning dizzily on the black marble basin, she looked at her own reflection in the mirror. She was looking romantically ethereal, but very pale, pale to her lips. And she hurt. Everywhere.

It took some time for the room to stop swaying around her. She sat weakly on the edge of the bath, also carved out of black marble, and took advantage of the privacy to loosen her gown, hoist up her chemise, and study her body.

There was a livid bruise on the top of each slender thigh, no doubt where the steering wheel had hit her, and various assorted scrapes and contusions in other places. But she had the sort of creamy, fine skin that marked easily, and it looked worse than it really was. She shuddered as she thought of what could have happened to her.

Damn that trucker, wherever he was. Whether deliberately or not, he had almost killed her with that stunt. She gave another wince at the thought that Cesare di Stefano had seen her naked body, and got to her feet again, this time a lot more carefully.

She washed and winced in about equal proportions, and was eventually feeling so weak and sick that she had to stop. She even caught herself sniffling a little in self-pity.

Maybe escaping from here today wasn't going to be so easy, after all. She was very fragile this morning; a good hard bump and she'd just fall to pieces.

She made her way very cautiously back, and crawled into bed, lying back against the pillows like a wan damsel in some Pre-Raphaelite painting, to wait for Vito's arrival. She looked dully round the room. It was quite beautiful, a symphony of whites and creams. Outside the three tall windows, oaks rustled and cypresses swayed gently in the breeze. Beyond, a deep blue sky framed a sunlit landscape.

Great weariness closed in on her, shutting out the

view, everything. She closed her eyes, feeling herself
drift away.

She awoke with a choking sensation of panic, as
though she were drowning, and cried out. As her eyes
flared open, the first thing she saw was the bronzed,
male face of Cesare di Stefano.

He was sitting on her bed, watching her. As she
stared at him in numbed confusion, he smiled.

'You are quite ravishing in your sleep, Claudia. You
would make a stunning fairy princess, with that deep
red hair and that translucent skin. How do you feel?'

She tried to sound lucid. 'F—fine. What time is it?'

He glanced at his watch. 'Three. You've been
asleep for a few hours.'

She stretched, brushing the hair away from her
eyes. 'Have my things come from the hotel?'

'Yes. Now that you're awake, Anna will put them
in your cupboards.'

'That won't be necessary,' Claudia said with grim
satisfaction. 'My fiancé is coming over this afternoon,
and I shall be leaving with him as soon as he arrives.'

'Ah, yes.' His expression was unreadable. 'A
pleasant young man, if rather dull. He seemed to have
the idea you were fit enough to go home with him.'

'Is he here?' she said, lighting up.

'He has just left.' Lines creased around his eyes as
he smiled. 'When he saw how sweetly you were
sleeping, he realised that the best thing was to leave
you in peace.'

'You sent him away?' she said incredulously.

He made a deprecating gesture. 'Quite the
contrary. Once I had explained how seriously ill you
were, he soon saw reason.'

'But I'm not ill in the slightest!' Frustration at having slept through Vito's visit made the tears boil up inside her. 'You—how could you do that? Why didn't you *wake* me?'

'You need all the sleep you can get.' He viewed her quivering mouth and wet eyes with indifference. 'Your boyfriend quite understood.'

'He's *not* my b—boyfriend. He's m—my fiancé.'

'How charming.' Cesare's voice was honeyed, the way you would talk to a six-year-old girl who'd announced her intention to marry the five-year-old boy next door. 'Please don't cry, *cara*. I think he intends to come and see you again tomorrow morning.'

'Tomorrow morning?' The thought of another night here was appalling. 'Why not later this afternoon? Or tonight?'

'Out of the question,' Cesare said implacably. 'I assured him it would be sensible to leave you to rest for a day or two.'

She glared at him, emerald eyes still glistening with tears. 'You mean you ordered him not to come back until tomorrow morning?'

'You make me sound like an ogre,' he purred. 'It was rather hard to follow him, as a matter of fact. He speaks very thick dialect, doesn't he?'

'Vittorio speaks fluent Italian,' she retorted.

'Ah. Perhaps he was shy.'

'I doubt it.' Mentally cursing Vittorio for letting himself be bullied by Cesare di Stefano, Claudia gulped back her tears, and set her mouth like an obstinate mare. 'Well, in that case, I'll have to call a taxi.'

'Quite impossible,' he said flatly. 'You are in no condition to travel anywhere.'

'I must!'

'You must not.'

'I have things to do——'

'You could collapse at any moment.' Strong brown fingers smoothed back the sheets she had tried to pull away. 'Your beloved Vittorio can wait.'

'It's not just Vito. I'm a businesswoman! If I don't meet my clients—just how long am I expected to stay cocooned in here like this?'

'Until the day after tomorrow, at least.'

'The day after tomorrow?' she repeated, aghast. 'That's impossible!'

'It is real, isn't it?' he asked calmly.

'What?' she asked, taken aback.

'The colour of your hair.' He reached out to touch a silky strand. 'It's always fascinated me. I'd be most disillusioned to learn that it was out of a bottle.'

'Of course it's real,' Claudia snapped.

'Remarkable,' he said. 'I've never seen a colour quite so rich. It's very, very beautiful. Quite autumnal.'

'You can't keep me here for two days,' she said, confusion making her stir restlessly in the sheets.

'Oh, but I can,' he promised smoothly. 'I'm an old friend giving succour. And you're much too weak to resist.'

She could only stare at him helplessly. He smiled, and reached into his pocket. The ear-rings he drew out were hers, pearl clips that her mother had given her last year. 'Yours, I think. Giuseppe found them in your car.'

'Yes,' she nodded, 'they're mine. They must have come off in the crash.'

'You see? Giuseppe may be a murderer, but not a thief. If he wouldn't take a pair of ear-rings, I doubt that he would take a life.' He leaned forward to fasten them on her ears. His knuckles brushed her cheeks as the gold clips nipped her earlobes like a lover's teeth. It was a disconcertingly intimate gesture, and the colour rushed to her pale cheeks. She pulled away as soon as she could.

'My engagement ring!' She'd just realised that her wedding finger was bare. 'Oh, no,' she said in distress, 'Vittorio's diamond—it's gone.'

'The diamond is safe,' he assured her. 'Anna took it off last night so the doctor could dress the scratches on your hands.'

'Can I have it back, please?'

'Of course. It's in my study for safekeeping. You shall have it soon.'

'I'd like it now!'

'There's no hurry.' He studied her with deep eyes. 'Do you ride, by the way?'

'Well . . . yes,' she said, taken aback by the unexpected question.

'Excellent.' He looked pleased. 'I should have guessed. Your muscle-tone is excellent. And those long, wonderful legs—I assume you took ballet as a child?' He ignored her hostile expression. 'As soon as you are fit enough, we must take the horses out. The weather is perfect for riding in these months—hot, but with a cool breeze.'

'*Signore,*' she said bitingly, 'I really wish you would get it into your head—I'm not staying! It's absurd to persist with this fiction that I'm here as your guest.'

'But you are my guest,' he said with intractable politeness. 'Surely you will allow me to offer a littlehospitality in return for the shock my driver gave you?'

She set her mouth. 'You can hardly imagine that it gives me any pleasure to be a prisoner here, after everything that's happened between us!'

Cesare's lids lowered. 'It would be foolish to get up

from a sick-bed out of mere contrariness. You must control your passionate nature for once, Claudia, and learn to resign yourself to what life throws in your path. What cannot be altered must be endured.'

Claudia felt a twinge of despair. Despite all his exquisite manners, the steel behind the velvet was utterly unyielding.

'You don't understand! For one thing alone, I'm due to fly back to London in a few days, and I've already missed several important appointments because of this accident. I'll be lucky if I don't have to put off my flight to fit everything in.'

'Put off your flight?' The grey eyes glittered. 'An excellent idea. I shall do it for you today.'

'No!' she yelped.

'I presume you flew Alitalia? Nothing could be simpler.'

'This is kidnapping——'

His eyes gleamed. 'Nonsense. But you haven't had a scrap of breakfast yet. No wonder you are fretful and off balance. Anna will bring you a cup of hot chocolate.' He reached for the bedside phone.

'Please,' she said tiredly, her head buzzing. 'Please, please, *please*.'

'Anything, my fairy princess,' he smiled.

'Could I have just a *tiny* cup of coffee?' She showed him with finger and thumb just how modest her requirements were. 'Just that much. Otherwise, I'm not going to be able to face the rest of my life.'

'How could I refuse such a request?' He relayed the order down the phone. Replacing the receiver, he glanced at her. 'Oh, and by the way—no more using the telephone, please.'

'Why not?' she protested, wide-eyed. 'I could get something done, at least, over the phone.'

'You don't seem to realise how ill you are,' Cesare said firmly. 'You were in shock last night. You didn't know where you were or what you were doing. So, no getting up, no phoning, and no arguing. If you are disobedient,' he said grimly, 'I'll have the phone taken out of your bedroom.'

'Then I *am* your prisoner,' she said angrily.

'My guest. And, to an extent, my responsibility. You've got to give your system time to recover, Claudia, or you'll be collapsing and having blackouts all over the place.'

She thought of that giddy spell in the bathroom, and stared at him glumly, lost for an answer.

Under the white silk of his sweater, the ripple of hard muscle was evident. He had the kind of lean-waisted, broad-shouldered figure that was supposed to be the perfect male physique, yet which you hardly ever saw in real life.

In fact, as he studied her with deep grey eyes, Claudia was reminded that he was one of the most physically impressive men she had ever seen. Not just attractive—he overwhelmed the senses with the kind of presence that only film stars had.

'Come, come,' he said, studying her expression. 'You have everything you need here. Why not accept *force majeure?*'

'I'm not used to being taken over like this,' she choked, close to tears again. 'Everything's suddenly so *awful*. I was so very happy until I bought that farm. Then everything in my life started going wrong . . .'

'You didn't buy it,' he reminded her inexorably. 'It still belongs to me.'

'After what your driver did to me,' she said tremulously, 'the least you could do is give me the place. That would go some way towards making reparation.'

'If I did that,' he smiled, 'you would walk out of my life, and I would never see those long, beautiful legs again. No, I think that is far too high a price to pay. Besides, think of the glamorous figure you'll cut in court—that red hair flaming among all the sombre black gowns. Of course,' he added with a wicked glint, 'there will be a few silver hairs in it by the time a settlement is reached.'

Claudia glared at him. 'I'll split the land with you. Fifty-fifty,' she ground out. 'But I keep the house.'

'Now, now,' he admonished. 'You're in no fit state to discuss business.'

'I can't be fairer than that,' she cried. 'Fifty-fifty's more than reasonable!'

'Not another word,' he said firmly, dark eyebrows coming down to reinforce the order. When he said something as though he meant it, rather than as a joke, the full force of his personality was rather overawing.

Sighing in miserable frustration, she let her hands drop back on the quilt. The reality of having no choice but to obey his wishes was starting to sink into her.

A tap at the door announced one of the maids, with a tray of coffee. The brew was hot and fragrant, and Claudia soaked it up like dry earth soaking up rain. 'For the first time,' she sighed in contentment, accepting a second cup, 'I feel human.' Her face clouded as she remembered Vito. 'I just wish I'd been awake to see Vito. He must be worried sick about me.'

'He seemed to be surviving,' Cesare said with a hint of irony. 'When are you planning to marry your accountant?'

'I've told you,' she said coldly, not liking that *your accountant*. 'As soon as that farm is ours.' She gave him a quick glance. 'If you and I could just come to some simple arrangement over the whole affair, I'd feel very much better.'

'May I ask why you didn't consult your fiancé before you launched into the purchase? He clearly knows all about money. No doubt he understands all about land, too.'

'He was in Switzerland. I wanted it to be surprise.'

'A surprise?' he said with a slight smile. 'I've always thought you a most remarkable young woman, *carissima*. Not given to stupid actions at all. What made you so impulsive this time?'

'I don't really know,' Claudia sighed, looking mournfully into her coffee-cup.

'Perhaps you were in too much of a hurry to get married,' he suggested drily. He studied her with reflective eyes. 'It strikes me as odd that someone as independent as you, with a highly successful business and a fulfilled life, should be so keen to marry, and throw it all away.'

'I don't intend to throw it all away. Besides,' she shrugged, 'perhaps my life isn't all that fulfilled, after all. And my busienss isn't exactly immense. Just two shops and a warehouse in London.'

'More than dear Vito ever dreamed of,' Cesare said smoothly.

She looked up suspiciously. 'What are you getting at?'

'Just that you're a very unusual and clever woman, Claudia.'

'Oh, I was lucky. I was so ignorant when I started that I sometimes think it's a miracle I survived at all.'

'You are too modest,' he said. 'That's a fault just as serious as being too proud, don't you think?'

She looked at him enquiringly. 'And what does

that mean, pray?'

But he just smiled that Cheshire-cat smile. 'An old saying of the di Stefanos.' He rose. 'And now, Anna is waiting to unpack your clothes. After which, I think Dottore Ortolani will be ready to see you.'

CHAPTER FIVE

'SO,' Vito demanded the next morning, when he came to the *palazzo* to visit her, 'just how long are you going to stay here?'

'Another night, at least. And the doctor thinks I should stay until the day after tomorrow, too.'

Vittorio's face darkened. 'Four days? I didn't stay in hospital that long when I broke my collarbone skiing!'

'I'm not exactly keen to be here myself,' she said pointedly. 'But the situation is awkward. Cesare is a very hard man to argue with. Besides——'

A smiling Anna entered the bedroom at that point, bringing a tray of coffee and pretty little *petits fours* for them.

'Thank you, Anna,' Claudia said gratefully, 'we'll pour for ourselves.'

With a curtsy to Vittorio, Anna melted away again.

'You seem to know all the servants' names,' he commented bitterly. 'You're quite the little duchess here. Does he encourage you to call him Cesare?'

'No, I just call him that. It's his name, and he doesn't seem to mind.' She picked the most tempting cake for him, and put it on his plate. 'Anyway, he calls me *Claudia*.' She imitated his pronunciation in a deep voice. 'He's not much older than we are. I don't think first-names are inappropriate.'

Vittorio sucked his teeth irritably. 'He is a duke.

You should not be so familiar.'

She snorted. 'I thought Italy was supposed to be a republic?'

'You don't understand anything,' he said crossly. 'I've warned you about him, Claudia. He's dangerous. He's not some gentlemanly fairytale knight who has chosen to rescue a damsel in distress. If he insists on keeping you here, then he will have some reason. And I'm afraid that the reason is all too clear.'

'The reason?'

'He has a bad reputation, as you very well know.'

'What kind of bad reputation?'

Vittorio rejected the *petit four* tersely. 'With women. And *you* have always had a weakness for him.'

'You're jealous!'

'I'm not jealous at all. I am angry,' he said sharply. 'You're utterly irresponsible, woman. This whole affair is going from bad to worse.' He put the delicate china cup down with a clack that made her wince. 'When are you going to stop acting like a spoiled brat?'

'I——'

'You went off and bought that farm without consulting me. You've already lost a fortune on it. Money which rightfully belonged to *us*. You refuse to take the logical path towards getting the money back. Instead, you insist on rushing here, against my advice, to see this man. Then you crash your car into a riverbed, trying to race a truckload of wine. And now you're stuck in his palace, in his bed, for as long as he sees fit, wearing something out of a French *bordello* that shows all your——' He waved his hand speechlessly.

'Yes,' she said urgently. 'But there's some point to it all. I was going to tell you my idea. I was thinking it over last night, and I've realised that this is an opportunity I shouldn't miss. While I'm here, as his guest, at least I can negotiate with him about the farm, and maybe reach a satisfactory arrangement of some kind.'

'You won't get anywhere with him.'

'I think I will! Yesterday, I suggested a fifty-fifty split—and he didn't say no. That would be better than nothing, wouldn't it? We'd still have our house, and over eight acres of vines. We could get married right away.'

'You're babbling like a girl,' he retorted stiffly. 'Can you not see how indelicate your situation is?'

'Indelicate? Don't be so Victorian,' she smiled.

'It is indelicate,' he insisted angrily. 'He has a hold over you. You want something out of him. And you are all alone in this house with him, in bed, wearing those things——' His expression indicated that he thought her chemise extremely sinful.

'Vito, this is childish,' she retorted, flushing.

'We Italians have different ways from you English,' he said, his eyes boring into hers. 'If you let him see your body, he will think you are offering yourself to him.'

The hot flush had spread down into her throat, and wouldn't go away. If Vittorio knew just how much of her body Cesare had really seen, he would explode! 'I assure you,' she said briskly, 'that I am not offering anything to Cesare di Stefano. I happen to think that this is as good an opportunity as any of getting a solution to our problems. I don't enjoy staying here, and I feel just as uncomfortable about it as you do, but while there's a chance of getting a compromise, without starting a lawsuit, I feel I must do the best I can.'

Vito glared at her, then snorted. 'I think you are mad, Claudia. But there's obviously nothing I can do to make you see sense, so I suppose I must give in graciously.'

'You'll see,' she soothed, reaching for his hand. 'It will all work out. I'm sure of that.'

'I'm not sure of anything,' he growled, accepting the touch of her fingers with ill grace.

A little cough from the door made them both turn. Anna was looking apologetic. 'Excuse me, *signorina*, but the doctor is here. Perhaps the gentleman would not object to retiring?'

'I'll go,' Vito sighed, rising to his feet. 'I'll see you again tomorrow morning, Claudia.'

'You won't forget to make those calls?' she reminded him, referring to several apologies she'd asked him to make to clients on her behalf.

'No, I won't forget.' He gave her a brief kiss, and left the room, looking very far from happy.

The doctor was a charming little man, whose old-fashioned bedside manner was somehow infinitely soothing. Despite his quaint air, he seemed to be a competent physician, and Claudia was inclined to respect his warnings that she should not exert herself in any way.

After his visit, however, she appealed to Cesare, who had come in to see her.

'I'll go mad with boredom! Stuck in bed for two more days! Can't I even walk round the *palazzo*?'

'No walking. Dottore Ortolani was quite specific. A pity, of course. You would enjoy the *palazzo*.'

'What I need is a little motorised golf-cart,' she sighed. 'Then I could get around without exertion.'

Cesare held up a lean, tanned hand. 'That has given me an idea. Great-Aunt Adele may have come to the rescue.'

'Great-Aunt Adele?'

'Yes.' He wore the ghost of a smile. 'She has something which will be very handy to you. I'll go and fetch it.'

'This is completely *ridiculous,*' she wailed as he folded the rug around her knees. 'You can't push me round in a *bathchair*! It's positively geriatric.'

'It's a very nice bathchair,' he soothed. 'Great-Aunt Adele is extremely fond of it. In fact, it's probably a valuable antique.'

'Great-Aunt Adele is a different shape from me.' She squirmed miserably in the wicker contraption until he slid another cushion down behind her. 'Cesare, I can't go out in this. Not when I can walk perfectly well.' She looked up at him with big green eyes. 'Your staff will laugh at me.'

'Not at all,' he promised gravely. 'You look deliciously romantic, like some Victorian consumptive not long for this world.'

'Oh, lovely.'

'Besides, you'll make a pleasant change from Great-Aunt Adele, who swings at them with her walking stick as she goes by.'

'I don't believe you,' she said, laughing despite herself. 'I'm sure Great-Aunt Adele doesn't even exist.'

His eyebrows arched. 'What a shocking sentiment. It's either this or bed, Claudia. Shall we go?'

'Oh, all right,' she capitulated with no good grace, and huddled down resentfully in the bath-chair as he wheeled it out into the corridor. She'd never felt so completely absurd in her life, being trundled along in an over-sized wicker basket on wheels, wrapped in a tartan rug, when she could probably have kept up with him in the hundred-yard dash.

Why did he enjoy making an idiot out of her? He took a keen relish in exposing her to the most ridiculous situations. She was too weak with him, damn it! Why did she *let* him do this to her?

'We'll begin with the rose drawing-room,' he decided, pushing her down the hall. 'An excellent setting for you. The general colouring ought to match your hair to perfection.'

'You sound as though you're planning to leave me there,' she said drily.

'Perhaps I am. You'd make a very exotic ornament.'

The house was huge, and the sensation of being wheeled smoothly along endless carpeted corridors was slightly dreamlike.

'Here it is,' he said at last. 'Do you know anything about architecture?'

'Very little.'

'I shall have to educate you.' He wheeled her into a vast room with a high, vaulted ceiling intricately decorated with plasterwork. The wallpaper was deep rose silk, and at each end was a great carved fireplace in pink marble. In between, islands of mahogany furniture rested on an ocean of Chinese carpet in shades of red.

'How beautiful!' she exclaimed, gazing around with wide eyes. 'How very lovely.'

'This room represents the peak of the Tuscan Palladian style,' he announced in a tour-guide's voice. 'Note the very fine Satsuma vases on the pedestals, the two Ming funerary urns on either side of the door, and the collection of Tung porcelain in the cabinet, which is Louis the Sixteenth.' He wheeled her round to face an exquisite female nude, carved out of white marble, which stood in an alcove framed by shelves of antique books. 'Bernini,' he commented. 'I thought she had the most beautiful breasts in the world. Until I saw yours.'

'I wish you would stop talking about that,' she said, flushing painfully. 'It's heartless.' There was a beautiful grand piano at the far end of the room, and she suddenly felt a great urge to play on it. 'I must get out of this chair,' she said impatiently. 'It's so frustrating to be wrapped up like this, unable to move. I'm bursting to walk around.'

'Sit.' A firm hand stopped her from rising. 'You're not strong enough.'

'But I *hate* this contraption!'

He came round to look at her, incredibly handsome, and with a glint in his grey eyes. 'How odd. You sounded exactly like Great-Aunt Adele just there. Perhaps it's the bathchair.'

'It's nothing of the sort,' she muttered, pulling the rug around her. 'I'm perfectly capable of walking. You just enjoy making a mug of me. It's horrible to be laughed at the whole time.'

'Am I laughing at you?' he asked, resting one fist on his hip to stare down at her. 'I don't think so.'

'You've been laughing at me since the moment I set foot in here,' she said with dignity. 'I want to walk, please.'

'It's a big place, *carissima*. You'd be worn off your feet even if you weren't in a delicate condition.' He pushed her into a big shaft of golden sunlight to admire the glow on her hair. 'There, I knew this room would suit you. Don't pout. Aren't you enjoying yourself?'

'In a wretched sort of way,' she shrugged. 'Well, if I can't walk, when are we going to talk about my farm?'

'My farm.'

'Our farm.'

'*Our* farm,' he said softly. 'Hmmm. I wonder whether I like that? Perhaps I do. We can talk about *the* farm as soon as you feel better.'

'I feel better now,' she said promptly, looking up at him with sunlit green eyes.

'No,' he corrected, 'I meant as soon as you feel better tomorrow. Do you know, your hair looked like fire in the sunlight? You could be a Renaissance angel, come to steal away my soul.'

'Very poetic.' His compliments made her feel distinctly awkward, bereft of a flippant reply. Vittorio never said things like that, in jest or seriously.

He smiled at her discomfort, and wheeled her more slowly through the grand chambers.

Finally, he opened a glass door and pushed her out on to a terrace over-arched by vines and wistarias. The fresh air was delicious, and the dappled sunlight was warm on her skin. He parked her next to the marble balustrade, so that she could look out over the magnificent view of the park, the lake, and the Tuscan countryside beyond. 'This is marvellous,' she sighed, unwrapping herself from her rug, and tilting her head back in bliss. 'Perhaps I needed a rest, after all. I've been working so hard lately.'

Cesare leaned on the balustrade beside her. Against the light, his figure was perfectly defined —lean and strong, with a swordsman's long legs. 'Your young man strikes me as a very traditional Italian male. Such men have very definite views about women. He will expect you to stop working once you are married.'

'Not altogether. I'll continue to buy my stock here in Italy, but I'll leave the day-to-day running of the shops to someone else. We've agreed on that.'

'Have you, now? You also realise that he will expect to have complete control over *your* money once you are married?'

'He may expect that,' she smiled, 'but he won't get it. The idea is silly.'

'No, *cara*. It may be unfair, even cruel, but it's not silly. It's a fact of life.' He tilted his handsome head at her. 'Have you ever read the Italian civil marriage service?'

'All that stuff about the man being the head of the family, and the woman having to obey him in everything?' She shrugged. 'No one takes that seriously.'

His eyes glittered. 'Try not to be too idiotic, Claudia. *Everyone* takes it seriously in Italy. Have you also read the bit which says that your money must be used to support your husband? Have you ever considered what that means?'

Claudia shut her eyes tiredly. 'I don't like the line you're taking, Cesare. It's ugly.'

'Do you love him?'

Claudia opened her eyes in surprise. 'That's a very strange question!'

'If you plan to marry the man, it's a perfectly natural question.' He was smiling, but his eyes were hard. 'Do you love him?'

'Of course I do.'

'Do you ever wonder whether he is the right man for you?'

'No,' she said, a flicker of anger running along her veins, 'I don't. And this is none of your business either, Cesare.

'I have just made it my business,' he said inflexibly. 'Unlike so many women, Claudia, you have known what it is to spread your wings and fly. You may come to hate the man who tries to cage you and take your freedom away.'

Too angry to even bother retorting, Claudia turned

her head stiffly away. How cruel, how hateful of him!

'Have I offended you?' he asked calmly.

'You've upset me,' she said with an effort. 'What the hell does it have to do with you? You don't know the first thing about Vittorio, and you only know *me* through business.'

'On the contrary, I see right into both your hearts,' he replied. 'It's a gift of the di Stefanos.'

'Really? I do appreciate the sudden interest in me and my fiancé. So kind.'

'Oh, I feel responsible, somehow. You don't have a father, do you?'

'I never knew him,' she said coldly. 'What has that got to do with anything?'

'Just this—that you know less than most women about men, and that you are probably looking for a father-figure.'

'Nonsense!'

'Tell me; this accountant of yours—are there any women in his family?'

'He's got a mother and two sisters,' she replied shortly.

'What are they like?'

'Very happy and very nice.'

'Always busy?' he suggested mildly.

'They're housewives,' she shrugged. 'Nothing extraordinary.'

'All too ordinary, in fact.' He slid his hands into his pockets, drawing his trousers taut across muscular thighs. 'They work all day long in the house, washing and cleaning. They're no strangers to working in the fields when it's necessary to save a labourer's wages. They also cook huge meals twice a day, and then do the washing up. When they aren't looking after their own menfolk, or their own children, they're looking after nephews and nieces. In fact, between the washing and the cleaning and the cooking and the children, they really don't have much time to do anything else. They don't go out and they don't have visitors, and they certainly don't run businesses.'

'My life won't be like that,' she said fiercely. 'I couldn't stand it, and nor could Vittorio.'

'I know you couldn't stand it,' he said silkily. 'The question is whether Vittorio, raised with that ideal of womanhood, could learn to stand *you*.'

'He knows what I'm like.'

'I very much doubt that.' He made a dismissive gesture. 'Of course, he desires you passionately. What man wouldn't? You are quite extraordinarily attractive, both physically and in your delightful character. You draw men to you. But does he feel anything deeper than a desire to get his hands on a rich, beautiful wife, whom he can exploit and abuse at will?'

She rose furiously from her bathchair, and swung her palm at his face. The blow caught him full on the cheek, so hard that her palm stung like nettle-rash.

His eyes blazed for a moment, the pupils black pinpoints. Then he smiled slowly, as though he had won some kind of secret victory. He stepped forward, and took her shoulders in his hands. She was too numb to resist as he drew her towards him, his mouth seeking hers.

The kiss was deliberately, shockingly intimate. It probed her womanhood with wicked expertise, his mouth warm and moist and confident, his tongue sliding between her lips as erotically as though they'd been lovers for years, and not casual acquaintances.

Too stunned to react, Claudia felt her heart turn over in her breast. Then, with a tiny whimper, she tried to struggle away. But he was as strong as steel, forcing his will on her, compelling her to remain. Her silk bedclothes were so thin that, when he drew her close to him, it was as though she were naked, the soft peaks of her breasts yielding againt the muscular wall of his chest, her thighs exposed to his hard loins.

Shock gave way to anger; and then, with utter perversity, anger gave way to a sudden flame of excitement. It was impossible to be indifferent to him; his manhood was so potent, like nothing she had known before. By the time the kiss ended, she was shuddering and weak, clinging to his strong neck as helplessly as though he'd just rescued her from drowning.

'I hate you,' she whispered weakly.

'No, you don't, he contradicted in a deep voice. 'You hate the truth. You're fascinated by me. You always have been. Exactly as I always have been fascinated by you.'

She looked up at him with eyes that were soft, frightened. She could feel the pulses leaping at her throat and wrists, as though she were about to faint.

'Let me go——'

'Not a chance,' he whispered. 'You've been in my blood a long time, Claudia. You're the most beautiful woman I've ever seen in my life!'

His eyes were deep grey pools in which you could drown; not cold, as she'd once thought, but warm, warm and passionate.

'This whole thing is crazy,' she heard a voice say with cool clarity, and realised that it was her own. 'Let me go, please.'

She pushed away from him determinedly, and took a step back. Or tried to. Her legs weren't there any more. Her legs had gone over to the enemy, and were folding up beneath her like rubber. She tried to reach for him to save herself, but it was too late.

She slid down to the floor, clung to his lean hips with her head against his belly for a few seconds, then slipped into a welcoming, peaceful black ocean.

She was only dimly aware of being carried back to bed in his strong arms. By the time she was coming to again, the doctor had been called.

'What have you been doing to her?' he clucked reprovingly. 'She was supposed to rest, not make a grand tour of the *palazzo!*' He prescribed some old-fashioned remedies which Claudia made a mental note not to touch, and got up to leave after half an hour.

'Look after her now,' he warned Cesare as he departed. 'She is delicate, Cesare. Rest and relaxation—remember!'

'I will,' Cesare promised.

Claudia looked up at him rather wanly when they were alone. 'There,' she said tiredly. 'See what you've done. I feel awful.'

'How awful?'

'Giddy and weak.'

He sat beside her, and smoothed the rich hair away from her brow. 'You shouldn't have slapped my face,' he said, his deep eyes smiling. 'It aroused my animal passions.'

She felt the colour touch her cheeks as she remembered that searing kiss. 'And you shouldn't have said those horrible things about Vito!'

'I spoke only the truth.' He laid a finger on her lips to silence the indignant retort that sprang to them. 'And no arguing. Remember what the doctor said—rest and relaxation. Roll on your stomach, and I'll rub your shoulders.'

She obeyed with a sigh, and closed her eyes as his fingers began gently massaging the tense muscles of .

HARLEQUIN DELIVERS FIRST-CLASS ROMANCE— DIRECT TO YOUR DOOR

Mail the Heart sticker on the postpaid order card today and you'll receive:

- **4 new Harlequin Presents® novels — FREE**
- **a lovely 20k gold electroplated chain — FREE**
- **and a surprise mystery bonus — FREE**

But that's not all. You'll also get:

Money-Saving Home Delivery

When you subscribe to Harlequin Reader Service®, the excitement, romance and faraway adventures of these novels can be yours for previewing in the convenience of your own home at less than cover prices. Every month we'll deliver 8 new books right to your door. If you decide to keep them, they'll be yours for only $2.24* each. That's 26¢ less than the cover price. And there is *no* extra charge for shipping and handling! There is no obligation to buy — you can cancel Reader Service privileges at any time by writing "cancel" on your statement or returning a shipment of books to us at our expense.

Free Monthly Newsletter

It's the indispensable insider's look at our most popular writers and their upcoming novels. Now you can have a behind-the-scenes look at the fascinating world of Harlequin! It's an added bonus you'll look forward to every month!

Special Extras — FREE

Because our home subscribers are our most valued readers, we'll also be sending you additional free gifts from time to time in your monthly book shipments, as a token of our appreciation.

OPEN YOUR MAILBOX TO A WORLD OF LOVE AND ROMANCE EACH MONTH. JUST COMPLETE, DETACH AND MAIL YOUR FREE OFFER CARD TODAY!

You'll love your elegant 20k gold electroplated chain! The necklace is finely crafted with 160 double-soldered links and is electroplate finished in genuine 20k gold. And it's yours free as added thanks for giving our Reader Service a try!

FREE OFFER CARD

4 FREE BOOKS

FREE GOLD ELECTROPLATED CHAIN

FREE MYSTERY BONUS

PLACE HEART STICKER HERE

MONEY-SAVING HOME DELIVERY

FREE FACT-FILLED NEWSLETTER

MORE SURPRISES THROUGHOUT THE YEAR — FREE

YES! Please send me four Harlequin Presents® novels, *free*, along with my free gold electroplated chain and my free mystery gift, as explained on the opposite page. 108 CIH CAPK (U-H-P-03/90)

NAME _____

ADDRESS _____ APT. _____

CITY _____ STATE _____

ZIP CODE _____

MAIL THE POSTPAID CARD TODAY!

Remember! To receive your free books, gold electroplated chain and mystery gift, return the postpaid card below. But don't delay!

DETACH AND MAIL CARD TODAY.

If offer card has been removed, write to: Harlequin Reader Service, 901 Fuhrmann Blvd., P.O. Box 1867, Buffalo, NY 14269-1867 her shoulders and neck.

'Mmmm,' she sighed dreamily after a few minutes, 'you're very good.'

'I practise on Great-Aunt Adele.' She could hear the smile in his voice.

'Does she really exist?' Claudia asked, her whole being focused on those strong, sure fingers.

'She's as real as—your claim to that farm.'

'Then she does exist!'

'Whatever you say.'

She felt him fold the sheets back to her waist, and lift the flimsy material of her chemise. She was too dreamy to object, and the touch of his palms on the naked skin of her back was a sensual delight. The massage was slow, rhythmical, easing all tension and pain out of her body. Languorous warmth was stealing through her veins, lulling her into dreams.

'You're putting me to sleep,' she protested drowsily.

'Exactly my intention.' She felt his lips touch the soft skin of her nape. 'I loved every second of that kiss, *cara*. I've been aching to do that for months. It was long, long overdue.'

She shivered, feeling the goose-flesh ripple up her back. 'Your skin is so fine,' he said softly. 'Smooth as marble, yet warm and fragrant. You should wear only the purest Chinese silk, Claudia. Nothing else can do your matchless complexion justice.'

'Far too extravagant for me,' she said in a dreamy voice. 'I can't afford Chinese silk.'

'I can,' he said, fingers spreading pleasure through her muscles. 'There are several bolts in a cupboard somewhere in the palace. I shall design you a gown. Now hush,' she heard his voice say. 'Just sleep.'

She slept the whole afternoon away. Her sleep was

deep and dreamless, and she was feeling so much better by early evening that Cesare allowed her to get out of bed to eat her supper.

A silver-service dinner for two, complete with glowing candles, had been laid out in an intimate little room near her bedroom. Through the arched windows, a full moon added a golden glow. She exclaimed in delight at the beauty of the setting.

'If only I was wearing something more appropriate than a dressing-gown,' she mourned, running her hands along the exquisitely fine linen of the tablecloth. He was wearing an immaculate dinner-jacket and black tie in her honour, and he looked utterly stunning.

'You're ravishing,' he assured her. 'Besides, in the candlelight, it looks exactly like a Marie Antoinette gown.'

'You're too kind,' she said disbelievingly. 'This silver is so beautiful. And the crystal!'

'It dates from the seventeenth century. Venetian, of course.' He poured wine into a glittering goblet. 'Now. You're the expert. Tell me about this Chianti.'

'All right.' She toasted him with a smile, inhaled the bouquet of the wine, then took a slow, reflective swallow.

'I'm disappointed,' he said, leaning back to watch her. 'Aren't you supposed to snort and gargle, and spit it out on the floor?'

'That's for amateurs.' She smacked her lips to please him. 'There. And to spit this out would be a crime.' She held it against the candlelight, admiring the ruby glow. 'It's an excellent, full-bodied *Chianti classico*. Very superior. The perfect accompaniment to any good, savoury food. I could sell a lot of this in London!'

'Indeed.' He studied her with dark eyes, in each of

which a tiny flame danced. 'You really think that's a good wine?'

'Yes.' She took another mouthful. 'The grapes are excellent. Where does it come from?'

'One of my properties,' he said casually. 'A little farm overlooking Lucca.'

'Beast!' she accused, and looked at the dark red wine mournfully. 'Does this really come from my farm?'

'My farm.'

'Oh, Cesare!' She looked tragic. 'This is an awful trick.'

'I thought you'd be interested,' he said with a wicked smile. 'The olive oil is equally good, by the way. You'll be able to taste that in the salad.' He nodded for the servants to bring in the first course.

'Was I dreaming,' she asked, toying with the wine glass, 'or did I hear you offer to design me a gown this afternoon, before I dropped off?'

'You weren't dreaming,' he assured her. 'I have some silk which is just perfect for you. It's been hanging around for a couple of years now, waiting for you to arrive.'

'What makes you collect something as recherché as Chinese silk?' she asked in some amusement.

'It's one of the materials I like to use most. I wasn't pulling your leg,' he added, catching her puzzled look. 'I'll design you a marvellous gown, believe me. That's my job.'

'You're a designer?' she asked in real surprise. 'A professional?'

'I'm rather surprised you haven't heard of me,' he said gravely, but she couldn't tell whether he was teasing or not.

'Really?'

'Really.'

'I would never have associated you with work of any kind,' she marvelled, 'let alone design-work.'

'Do I seem so effete?' he asked drily.

'No,' she admitted. 'But you must be sickeningly rich. Most people who live in palaces avoid any form of work like the plague. What do you design?'

'Anything,' he shrugged. 'Any material from stainless steel to Chinese silk. Furniture, lighting, coffeepots, sports cars, industrial machines, kitchen tiles —anything and everything that my clients or my inspiration bring to me.' The food had arrived, and he waved the servants away so that he could serve her himself. 'In your case, I feel inspired to be a fashion designer.'

'You never cease to amaze me,' Claudia said, shaking her head. 'I never had the faintest idea. Are you very famous?'

'In my own circles, yes,' he said immodestly. 'However, the man in the street usually doesn't care who designs the car he drives or the cup he drinks his coffee from, as long as the shapes please him.'

'I'm dying to see something you've designed,' she said eagerly. 'Have you got a studio here?'

'Yes,' he nodded, 'and an office in Florence. But after dinner you're going straight back to bed. I'll show you the studio when you're well enough to walk around. Maybe tomorrow. Now, eat your food before it gets cold.'

The meal was superb, and Cesare was a bewitchingly charming host. He had that rare talent of being able to make her laugh until her sides ached, and yet he was no buffoon. His wit was rapier-sharp, deadly, and he could deliver the most devastating satirical comments on anything which annoyed or displeased him.

And tonight she was reminded of just what a great

deal of things seemed to annoy them in common. Perhaps that was why she'd always found him so entertaining; the things he satirised were exactly the things she felt most needed satirising.

In all the months she'd known him, and on all the occasions she'd met him, she'd been aware of that affinity between them. But what had happened between them over the past few days had intensified that feeling into something much more potent than a mere spark. The attraction between them was intoxicating now, like some exotic flower which had only been a bud until that kiss, and which now had opened fully, to drug her with its perfume and dazzle her with its colours.

By the time they were getting to the end of the meal, consisting of more wine, with some delicious local fruits and cheese, the conversation had come around to things they enjoyed in common.

One of them, it seemed, was classical music, in which Claudia had been trained for several years.

'You sing?' he exclaimed with real pleasure.

'Strictly amateur,' she said, now inexplicably shy. 'My mother used to be a fine soprano, but she gave it up when she got married. She wanted me to study music, so I took piano and singing until I was nineteen. But I wouldn't dream of subjecting you to my caterwauling.'

'But I insist!' His expression told her he meant it. 'There's a Bechstein in the rose drawing-room. I'll have them bring the coffee there. And you shall not get a drop until you've sung for me.'

'You really do have the Borgia touch,' she smiled.

He rose from the table, and lifted the heavy silver candelabrum from the centre of the table. 'This is much more aesthetic than electric light. Come.' Taking her arm, he led her to the rose drawing-room.

By the light of the candelabrum, the beautiful room took on a special mystery. Its eight tall candles sent flickering shadows dancing across the marvellously intricate ceiling, shadowing the far corners in soft darkness. Cesare showed her the music cabinet, and went to lift the lid of the grand piano while she started leafing through the sheets.

'A lot of this is too difficult,' she mused. 'And this is too sentimental. Hmmm. Not many people know these Brahms *lieder*. Do you like them?'

'They're among my favourite songs,' he nodded.

'Mine too.' She smiled into his eyes. 'Do you know this song?'

He glanced at the title. 'Very well,' he said quietly. 'But I warn you—I fall in love with anyone who plays that.'

She glanced at him quickly, then laughed. 'I'll have to take that risk. This is the only one I can guarantee. I did it for my last exam.'

For answer, he took the music from her, and unfolded it on the piano. 'I'll turn the pages,' he said. 'Can you see all right?'

'Fine.' She sat at the gleaming keyboard, and tried to few experimental chords. The result was the unmistakably rich tone of a perfectly tuned Bechstein. 'This is a concert instrument,' she marvelled. 'You're too rich for your own good, Cesare!'

'The instrument was my mother's,' he answered gently. 'I bought it for her a few years before she died.'

'Oh, Cesare, I'm sorry,' she said remorsefully. 'She must have been a fine musician.'

'She was a very gifted soprano,' he smiled. 'Like your mother.'

'Really?' She looked uncomfortably at the beautiful piano, rather wishing it was a more ordinary instrument. 'Perhaps I'd better not play on it, then,' she said hesitantly. 'I don't want to make a mess of the Brahms . . .'

He touched her cheek with warm fingers. 'You won't,' he said softly. 'Play, *carissima*.'

Feeling distinctly nervous, Claudia flexed her fingers, took a deep breath, and began.

The moment she started, she knew it was going to be all right. Her playing was faultless, and her voice rose into the silence sweet and clear. Perhaps it was the room, or perhaps it was the ambience, but her voice even seemed to take on an extra richness it seldom had on other occasions.

She was well aware of his eyes fixed intently on her face as she sang, yet that didn't bother her, either. She just wanted to give him some pleasure in return for the pleasure he had given her tonight.

Knowing that he loved the song, she delivered it clean and pure, without frills or excessive emotion. The beautiful music seemed to flow all around them, locking them in its spell.

When she played the last sad notes, and let her hands drop into her lap, he was still staring at her in silence. Uncertainly, she met his eyes. They were deep and warm, and the expression in them made her heart miss a beat.

"Thank you,' he said simply, reaching for her hand. 'That was very beautiful.'

She coloured at the praise. 'Would you like me to play another?'

'No. I was unfair to make you play at all—you are tired. And I want to keep listening to that song in my heart for a while.'

'You say some lovely things,' she said, shutting the lid of the piano. She rose, and stood facing him. In the soft light of the candles, his face seemed more hand-some than ever.

'I warned you about that song,' he said, his eyes still holding hers.

'Have you fallen in love with me?' She tried to smile, but it was a rather shaky smile for some reason.

'Oh, yes.' His voice raised goose-flesh all along her bare arms. 'But then, I knew I would.'

'Cesare,' she rebuked uneasily, 'you should never make jokes like that.'

'Do you think I am joking?' he asked softly.

'Of course I do!'

His answer was to cup her face in his hands, and kiss her mouth.

This time the kiss was intoxicatingly sensual, with none of the violence of this morning. It was the climax of the spell, the climax of the magical beauty of the whole evening.

Claudia melted against him helplessly as she felt his palms slide hungrily down her flanks and hips, move up the slender line of her spine in a slow, delicious caress, pressing her closer against him. His lips were brushing her eyelids and temples, gentle as butterfly's wings, exploring, caressing the scented, quivering skin.

God, he was all man! What he was doing to her with his mouth and hands was wickedly, criminally erotic; and her response was almost animal in its feminine intensity.

She was an engaged woman, a guest in a stranger's house. Yet shame had no power over her. Insane though she knew it was, wicked though she might be, she could not resist. It was such heaven to be held like this, kissed like this, made love to by such a man.

Slowly, without any volition on her part, her hands raised to caress his face in return, one hand spreading to cup the lean, hard angle of his jaw and cheekbone, the other running sensually through his thick, dark hair, the crisp waves enfolding her fingers as though returning her caress.

And surrender brought with it an exquisite reward, the deep shudder of pleasure that was like the unleashing of some new chemical in her bloodstream. He intoxicated her, thrilled her. She'd never felt like this with any man in her life before—not Vittorio, nor any of the men who'd kissed and held her. This was a pure, all-encompassing pleasure that was as irresistible as drowning, as exhilarating as tumbling through space.

Any thoughts of Vito were lost in the smell of Cesare's skin and hair, the body of this tall, potent stranger whose heart she could feel pounding against hers.

He released her mouth at last, but not her body, and looked down at her with brilliant eyes. 'Are you going to faint again?' he asked huskily.

She shook her head, feeling the length of his body hard and close against her own, his arms holding her tight, the way she'd always dreamed a man would one day hold her.

'There was always something special between us,' he said quietly, 'wasn't there, *cara?*'

She nodded, unable to speak.

'I knew that passion was possible between us,' he went on, staring deep into her eyes. 'But this——' He shook his head slowly. 'This is deeper and stronger than I ever expected. You know that this can be no mere flirtation, Claudia. Not between such as you and I.'

She could only stare up at him with whirling emotions.

'What am I going to do?' she whispered, almost too low for him to hear. 'What am I going to do?'

There was a discreet clink from behind them, and they parted. The servants were setting out the coffee things on a table, and the moment was over.

But she knew it would come again.

CHAPTER SIX

TURNING blissfully under the shower the next morning, Claudia felt that her head had cleared at last. After a troubled night of wild dreams, she had woken feeling composed, calm, and in control of herself again. It was the feeling she always got when a thunderstorm had washed away the muggy, hazy air, leaving the view unobstructed and transparent to the eye.

She'd been in a kind of madness yesterday and last night. That was the only explanation. She'd been a fool from the start.

And what a complete fool she had been. As she soaped her slender body under the stinging jet, it occurred to her that she hadn't been seeing things this clearly for a long, long time. Buying that farm had been the first step into madness. Looking back, it was incredible that she could have been so thoughtless, that she could have taken such a wild gamble.

Coming to this palace to confront Cesare had been the second mad step. She should never have done it. She should have believed Vittorio when he'd warned her that di Stefano was a dangerous man.

And not slowing down to let that truck overtake had been the third, almost fatal, error of judgement. All three actions showed the same blind lack of foresight. All three showed the same headstrong, wilful character.

Maybe it really was time she settled down, and became a docile Italian wife to Vito Brunelli. Being a crazy English fiancée had its perils.

And small wonder that Cesare di Stefano regarded her as fair game, both sexually and financially. She'd made an utter ass of herself in front of him; her stupidity had allowed him to feast his eyes on her naked body; and the natural consequence had been a determined attempt on her virtue.

She thought with a shudder of the wild dreams she'd had in the night. Dreams in which she and the Duke of Ferraro had committed the most abandoned acts together, sprawled on a vast crimson sheet, while the dark face of Vito had looked on grimly from a corner of the room.

Morning had thankfully veiled the details to a large extent, but the guilt lingered on like an old ache. She'd never had such erotic dreams about a man she hardly knew.

But it was only her stunned state after the accident that had made her respond like that. She loved Vittorio Brunelli very much, and no other man—not even one as devastatingly attractive as Cesare di Stefano—could have overwhelmed her with such ease if she hadn't been half dazed with shock.

Yesterday, on the terrace, and last night in the rose drawing-room, she had given way through weakness and folly. Oh yes, he was attractive, she'd always known that. But not that attractive. She could control herself better than he could—a woman always had that advantage.

Today, she vowed fervently, the game would be played to *her* rules. And if she couldn't make him resign all claims to that farm by the time she next saw Vittorio, then she wasn't the woman she thought she was!

Feeling deliciously clean and refreshed, Claudia stepped out of the shower and dried herself. It was lovely to be rid of the frowsty feeling that came of lying in bed all day. She examined the bruises on her thighs and arms. They had darkened, and were still very tender, but from now on they would fade. She had been very, very lucky.

Still naked, she turned to the full-length mirror, and began brushing her hair into thick, gleaming swathes, planning the arguments she would use on Cesare di Stefano later today. She felt ready to take anything and anyone on.

In the carved black marble setting of the bathroom—God, how rich was Cesare?—her body took on an almost translucent glow. Reflected in the glass, she looked exactly like what Cesare had once called her—a fairy princess.

The rich mass of her copper-beech hair, tumbling over her shoulder as she combed it out, emphasised the pale creaminess of her skin. Her breasts were exquisite; small and high, they moved tautly to the movements of her arm, the jutting nipples a flagrant invitation to a lover's kiss. The slender grace of her body seemed almost fragile, until you noticed the firmness of her figure, the swell of delicate but strong muscles at thighs, stomach and back. She *had* taken ballet, until well into her teens, and, though too tall to have ever danced on the stage, Claudia retained a ballerina's litheness of line and movement.

Wrapping a towel round her torso, she pushed through into the bedroom, humming to herself.

And at that moment, Cesare di Stefano was

coming in through the opposite door.

She stopped short in embarrassment, hands flying to secure the all-too-small towel over her nakedness. But he merely smiled benignly.

'How appropriate,' he purred. 'I'm so glad you haven't dressed yet.' He was wearing dark trousers and a fitted linen shirt, a fine burgundy pullover slung carelessly over his shoulders. He was heart-stoppingly handsome, darkly and completely male. Under one arm he was carrying a gleaming bolt of what looked like black silk. He patted it with his free hand. 'The Chinese silk I told you about. This one seemed to match your colouring best.'

'I'm getting dressed,' she said pointedly, wondering whether to retreat back into the bathroom and lock herself in.

'You look wonderful this morning.' His eyes were warm and appreciative as he came over, and bent down to plant a firm kiss on her flinching mouth. 'And you smell heavenly, as always. Did you sleep well?'

'Fine,' she said stiffly. 'Cesare, I want to get dressed——'

'Did you dream of me?' he enquired, looking down at her from under brooding lids. The question made her flush, but she shook her head firmly.

'I dreamed of nothing.'

'Liar,' he said softly. 'You persist in avoiding the truth, but you forget—I see right into your heart, *carissima*. Tell me, what do you think of this?'

He unravelled the bolt as he spoke. The silk shimmered like something magical, almost too fine to be real. The jet-black background was decorated with tiny flowers in vivid, almost metallic colours. 'It's lovely,' she said, cautiously extending a hand to touch it.

'Yes,' he nodded. 'I bought it myself, in Shantung. On you, it will be more than lovely. It will draw the very breath of life. Let us see. Take off your towel, *cara.*'

'Don't be silly,' she retorted.

'Let me help you——'

'No!' she said in alarm.

'Come, come,' he said smoothly, one eyebrow arching. 'You forget that I am no stranger to the beauty of your body. We must see whether the silk really suits you or not.'

'Cesare,' she pleaded nervously, 'you're very kind, but I honestly don't want this silk. I'd never wear it——'

'Of course you would wear it.' He pulled the red pullover from round his neck, and tossed it on to a chair. 'Your wardrobe has never matched your face and figure. It's high time you started wearing clothes that were really designed for you, and not bought off some peg. Let me show you what I mean.' His eyes met hers with that irresistible glitter of command. 'Take off your towel.' As she hesitated miserably, he sighed in exasperation. 'At the moment, my dear Claudia, I am far more interested in you as a designer than as a lover.' He held the silk up as a screen between them. 'I won't even look, if it offends you. Drop the towel.'

Unhappily, she let the towel slip away, using her arms to cover her breasts, and stood naked before him. With a grunt of satisfaction, Cesare pressed the silk against her, and wound a length of it around her torso. 'Lift your arms, for God's sake. There.'

She winced away from the touch of his hands through the silk, but it didn't take long. He pulled

the material tight around her, and let the rest of it
tumble to the carpet. Stepping back, he tilted his
dark head on one side. 'Hmmm,' he mused. 'I
should have known. That's even better than I'd
hoped.'

She glanced at herself in the long cheval-glass by
the window. The black silk gleamed as it hugged her
body, making an impossibly exotic figure of her.
The effect, even without a single stitch or scissor-cut,
was stunning. It was so fine that it seemed to cling
like a second skin, her breasts curving provocatively
against the material. The rich colour suited her
colouring to perfection, turning her into an oriental
empress.

'It *is* lovely,' she murmured, smoothing the stuff
over her thighs, and shifting her stance.

'You see? My judgement is infallible.' He walked
round her with that panther-like grace, studying her
from every angle. 'Superb,' he said softly. 'A dream
of beauty, and irresistibly erotic into the bargain.
Stand like that for a moment, please.'

He stepped back, and took a slim gold pen from
his pocket. In a small notepad, he began making
rapid, confident sketches.

'There, I think that will give the tailors enough to
go on.' He put the pen and pad down, and came
over to her.

She shuffled over to the bed in her cocoon of silk,
and looked down at the sketch he had made. It was
unmistakably professional work, the bold lines
suggesting an evening dress that would be dazzling
when it was completed. He had even caught the
typical way she stood, and the mass of her Titian
hair, so that the faceless female figure in the sketch
was unmistakably Claudia.

'You *are* gifted,' she acknowledged. 'You promised to show me some of the things you've designed this morning.'

He smiled into her eyes, and used both hands to draw the heavy, lustrous hair away from her face. 'Of course. But supposing they make you fall in love with me?'

'Are they that beautiful?'

'Dangerously beautiful,' he said softly, his eyes dropping to her mouth. 'Like you, *cara*.'

She was suddenly aware of her nakedness under the flimsy silk covering, which—to make things worse—was starting to fall open at the back.

'Y—you said you were only interested in me as a designer,' she reminded him nervously, moving back.

'I was. But now I have finished designing.' The touch of his mouth was electric, making her draw back. But he cupped her face in his hands to immobilise her, and kissed her lips with slow pleasure, as though it was something he had been aching to do for hours, his thumbs massaging her cheeks and temples in a way that made her senses reel. 'Mmm,' he growled softly, 'you taste like summer, of strawberries and fresh meadows.'

'I—I think I'll get dressed now,' she said, her heart pounding at his closeness. But the wretched silk, not having any fastenings, was slipping inexorably away from her smooth shoulders, leaving her back totally naked. It was only the pressure of her elbows to her sides that left her any decency at all.

With amused eyes, he bent to touch the creamy skin of her left shoulder with his lips. 'How delicious you look. You could pose for Aphrodite, surprised at her bath.' With sensitive fingertips, he traced the sloping line of her shoulders, up the side of her neck, to the shell-like curve of her ear. 'Such wonderful lines,' he said softly, almost to himself. 'Like something sculpted by the sea and the wind. Why do I spend hours at my drawing-board, when such lines are here, under my very eyes?'

He drew her close, and she found she could not resist as he sought her mouth. All those resolutions in the shower, all that self-knowledge, were vanishing like mist in the sun. With wanton eagerness, her lips were opening for him, her soul aching for the caress of his tongue. And at her invitation it came with added potency, licking the inner sweetness of her lips, probing her own tongue with insistent, soft-hard pressure, until she could not but respond.

With a whimper, she melted against him, her arms reaching round his neck. She felt his hands claim her naked back, caressing and moulding her skin.

She had never known kisses like this, never in her life. That any man could use his mouth with such shocking intimacy was a revelation to her; Cesare's lips and tongue were instruments of erotic pleasure, teaching her to respond with an abandon she had never experienced before. Not once had Vittorio kissed her like this; she knew in her heart that he wasn't capable. Only a man like Cesare could do this to her.

Excitement was unfolding inside her like a great pair of wings, ready to take flight into perilous, high regions that frightened her, yet drew her on. How could she resist him? He was so beautiful, so male, he knew so very much about her.

He was right, she thought giddily. He *did* see into her soul. He knew what she wanted, he knew how to kiss her and touch her the way she'd always dreamed a man would one day do.

'My beloved,' he whispered, 'I don't know how long I can go on without possessing you. You have stopped me from sleeping! I can no longer shut my eyes without seeing your face. I cannot smell a rose without smelling the perfume of your skin. And when I watched the dawn this morning, it seemed to me that your bright hair was spread out across the eastern sky, like the blood of the sun itself . . .'

She let him guide her with gentle hands, sinking down on to the bed with him. 'You're a seducer,' she whispered dreamily, looking up into that magnificent face. 'You spin these words like a web, to trap me into something that is very, very wrong.'

'What is so wrong?' he demanded, caressing the arched line of her throat.

'Making me betray Vittorio is wrong. You know that.'

'To let you marry him would be far worse,' he said grimly.

'But I'm going to marry him. I'm engaged to him.'

'You can break your engagement.'

'I've given my word! And anyway, I love him! I love him!'

'Insanity,' he said scornfully. 'He is pleasant enough, but dead wood, all the same. He will never inspire any great feeling in you. Or you in him, for that matter.'

'How can you say such things?'

'I can see right to the grasping heart of the man. He wants your money more than he wants you,

Claudia. Think what a glorious catch you must seem to him—wealthy, sophisticated, beautiful. Yet you can never make him happy. Nor he you.'

'Stop,' she whimpered, feeling the maelstrom inside her. 'You frighten me!'

'You cannot marry Vittorio. I will not permit it.'

'It's not for you to permit or forbid,' she said shakily. 'I've agreed to be his wife. He has given me his ring.'

He laughed shortly. 'I threw that ring into the lake this morning, at dawn.'

'You didn't!' she gasped, a pang of horror making her sit up.

'Perhaps a fish will swallow it,' he said ironically, 'and perhaps you will catch the fish one day. But that is the only way you will ever see that ring again.'

'I don't believe you,' she said in awe.

'Believe me, *carissima*. I never say things in vain.'

With dismay, she realised in her heart that Cesare was telling the truth. She could see it in her eyes. It was unbelievable, but he had done it. He had thrown Vittorio's diamond into the lake!

She stared at him, green eyes so wide that the white encircled them completely. Then, irresistibly, she felt the giggle rise up inside her. He grinned in response, white teeth flashing.

'That's how easily an engagement can be broken,' he said quietly.

'You're mad,' she said, swallowing her shocking moment of mirth. 'What in heaven's name am I going to tell him this morning?'

'Tell him the truth. That you never loved him.'

'I did! I do!'

'*Piccola idiota.*' He kissed her almost violently,

cupping her chin in strong fingers, hurting her mouth. She was almost shocked by the force of his onslaught, yet she exulted in it too, exulted in his strength, and the depth of his desire for her.

The black silk slid away from her breasts, exposing them to his touch. Hungrily, his mouth closed over her nipples, his teeth biting gently, sweetly. Her fingers knotted themselves in his hair, drugged lids closing over her eyes. It was a pleasure almost too sweet to be borne, his lips seeming to suck the very soul out of her, until she moaned his name out softly, her head dropping on to his, her deep red hair cascading all around both their faces. 'Why did I ever come here?' she moaned in anguish. 'This is torment, Cesare. I must get away from you . . .'

'I'll bolt you in,' he growled, 'and throw the key after Vittorio's ring.'

She hardly knew whether he was teasing her or not, but his words sent a thrill of mingled delight and terror through her heart.

'You cannot leave,' he said huskily. 'You cannot even think of it. We have so much to do together, so much to know about each other.' His fingertips trailed across her breasts, touching the nipples that still glistened moistly from the caress of his tongue. 'You were meant for me, and we've both been too blind to see it.'

'Stop!' she gasped, trapping his hand between her own. But, treacherously, she found herself smoothing his fingers out over the firm mound of her breast, so that her nipple jutted into his warm palm. 'You can't believe that!'

'Don't you believe in destiny?'

'No,' she denied, looking up at him with cloudy eyes. 'I believe only in myself.'

'Excellent,' he smiled, cupping her breast and drawing his thumb slowly across the aching peak. 'Then look into your heart, my love, and ask yourself what you are doing here'

The bedside phone chirped softly, and he turned to lift the receiver. 'There,' he smiled, after a moment, replacing it, 'breakfast is being served on the terrace. Let's go and have it. Your fiancé will be here in an hour.'

'Oh, yes,' she said with a brittle laugh. 'Fainted clean away. When I woke up, the dear old doctor was tut-tutting over me, prescribing camomile and valerian.'

'I see,' Vittorio said stiffly. 'You should not have got out of bed.'

'I thought I'd be safe in a bathchair,' she said, reaching for his hand.

'Bathchair?' he repeated the English word, and carefully disentangled his fingers from hers. 'May I ask what a bathchair is?'

'*Una poltrona a ruote,*' she translated for him.

'Such as they use for old women?' he enquired, dark eyes narrowing scornfully.

'Yes. Isn't it too ridiculous?'

He didn't find it too ridiculous. 'I thought it had something to do with the bath—as in taking your clothes off and washing.'

Absurdly, the colour rushed to her face at the mention of nakedness, making her seem stupidly guilty. 'Nothing like that,' she assured him with another breathless laugh. 'They're called bathchairs because they're supposed to come from Bath, in England, which used to be a resort for elderly invalids—oh, what are we talking about such silly things for?'

'I don't think it's silly,' Vittoria said shortly. His eyes dropped to her left hand. 'Where is your engagement ring?'

There could hardly have been a greater contrast between their moods this morning. Claudia was almost feverish, alternating between bright laughter and near-tears. Two red spots burned in her pale cheeks, giving her an almost consumptive look. Sometimes she felt so exhausted that it was all she could do not to sink back against her pillows and close her eyes, and sometimes her whole body seemed to quiver with restlessness, as though she wanted to leap up and run from this beautiful bedroom into the brilliant morning outside.

And Vittorio was at his worst. Leaden, suspicious, he was neither sympathetic to her tears nor amused by her jokes. His eyes had a grimly accusatory look.

'I've told you,' she sighed, 'they took it off the night of the accident. Cesare has it safe somewhere. I'll ask him for it when he comes in again . . .'

'I do not understand why he should have taken it off in the first place. You have been here three days already. Surely you are recovered now? And if you are not, you must come to my house. Mamma will look after you better than anyone here.'

'I don't think I could face the drive,' she said truthfully. 'Passing out like that was quite alarming. I've never felt quite so helpless and strange before. Don't look at me like that, my love. There's nothing I can do! The doctor insists I stay in bed, and I really don't feel very strong.'

'You should make the effort,' he said without much sympathy.

'But I feel so awful,' she pleaded. 'Don't bully me.'

His voice rose, charged with passion. 'We're supposed to be engaged! Supposed to be getting married! Don't you care what people are saying about you? Don't you understand that you're making a spectacle of yourself *and* me?'

The colour left her cheeks. 'Oh, Vittorio, I'm sorry.'

'You phoned me the morning after the accident, insisting that I come over at once and take you away,' he went on, letting his anger out in a tirade. 'You insinuated that the Duke had tried to murder you. I almost called the police, do you know that? Thank God I didn't make such a fool of myself. Then, when I arrive, I find you fast asleep. I'm told by di Stefano that I've wasted my journey, and that you cannot be disturbed.'

'I'm so sorry,' she repeated helplessly. 'I really did want you to take me away. And for a while I did think Cesare tried to kill me—it was the after-effect of the crash, I think. I must have been more shocked than I thought——'

'Yesterday morning,' he went on grimly, 'I offered to take you home again. You refused, saying you were far too ill to be moved.' His eyes flashed like obsidian. 'Then minutes after I leave, it seems you are up and about in your *bathchair,* being pushed around by the man who is supposed to have tried to kill you, exerting yourself to the extent that you pass out on the terrace. And this morning you tell me you are too ill to come to my house, which is the only right and proper thing to do in the circumstances! How am I to explain this situation to my mother and my sisters? How can I answer the questions they ask me? It's not good enough, Claudia. You're not considering me at all!'

She felt utterly wretched, and not just because she was piercingly guilt-stricken. Vittorio had never said things like that to her before, and they hurt with unexpected keenness. It was as though he had sensed that something strange had happened between her and Cesare di Stefano. But how could he have done?

She wanted to reassure him that he had nothing to be upset about.

But she knew in her heart that he had. Those kisses between her and Cesare—nothing like that had ever happened to her in her life. She had a fleeting, burning memory of lying with him, near naked, on this very bed this morning. Had she been engaged to someone other then Vito, she might have told him everything, talked it over. But, with Vittorio, that was impossible. She was forced to be silent.

Could she really swear that her desire to stay here was purely for the farm?

Yes! She hadn't wanted those kisses. Cesare had kissed her, not the other way round. He'd taken advantage of her weakness and her helpless position.

Yes, but she had enjoyed every burning second of them.

And yet, that wasn't her fault! It was as though Cesare had cast some spell over her, making her do things that were against her deepest inner will. Maybe she *should* get out of here, get as far away from the dangerous presence of Cesare di Stefano as possible . . .

But how could she? Vittorio was right. Cesare *did* have a hold over her.

Vito drew a breath shaky with anger. 'Enough is enough, Claudia. You must come home with me.'

'I can't go yet, Vittorio. I can't. I *must* get some kind of answer out of him about the farm.'

He exclaimed in Italian. 'You will get nothing out of him!'

'I will!' she said urgently. 'It's the only way out.' She shook the glowing mane of her hair back restlessly. 'Cesare will agree to some compromise in the end. We can't afford to go to court over this, and I don't think he wants to, either. Maybe tomorrow I'll be able to talk him into a deal. You know how persuasive I can be. Even sixty-forty, if it comes to that.'

'He's turned you down once,' Vittorio pointed out angrily.

'He's coming round,' she promised. 'What other chance will we have? I stand to lose tens of thousands of pounds, remember! And getting an agreement means being able to get married this year. Please trust me,' she said, raising tired eyes to his. 'I know what a fool I've been. But I must at least try and salvage something out of the mess I've made. If you don't think I can be trusted that far, then perhaps you don't trust me enough to be my husband. I'm sorry.'

Vittorio's expression tightened. 'Of course I trust you. I'm just hurt by what other people say and think.'

'Like who? Your family?'

'They find you hard to understand sometimes,' he shrugged. 'You are very different from Italian woman. My mother . . .' He shook his head darkly. 'You must understand that this kind of thing must never happen once we are married.'

'It never will,' she promised. 'Oh, it never will! Hold me, Vittorio.'

He took her in his arms with a sigh, and she clung to him for comfort. It was good to feel his arms round her. She and Vittorio were physical with one another to the extent of hugs and kisses, and sometimes more. But they had never made love. Not even when they'd been sorely tempted.

Claudia was not a virgin. She had never told him that, though she felt he had probably guessed—just as she had guessed that he was not a virgin, either. It was not a subject they ever discussed. From the moment they had agreed to marry, there had been a tacit assumption that they would wait until their wedding-night. Everything between them, partly because of the watchful proximity of his mother, had been as pure as the driven snow.

But this sexual jealousy was something new between them. He had never suspected her of any kind of infidelity before, even though they often had to spend weeks apart, he in Italy, she in London.

'I hope I'm not interrupting anything.'

They pulled apart as the purring voice came from the door. Cesare was watching them with that slow, ironical smile, his grey eyes veiled by heavy lids.

Vittorio rose to his feet, colouring angrily at the interruption. 'We were just talking.'

'So I see.' Cesare came into the room, and looked down at Claudia's pale face. 'You look tired, *carissima*.'

'I'm fine,' she said, trying not to wince at that *carissima*. It was a very intimate term of affection for a stranger to use, and it had made Vittorio's face turn to stone.

'You must not tire yourself.' Uninvited, he sat

beside her, and smoothed the thick, glossy hair away from her forehead. She felt her skin flaming. After what had just passed between her and Vittorio, this was hardly helpful! She drew away from him hotly.

'I'm not tired yet, thank you. And I was enjoying a little *private* conversation with my fiancé!'

His eyes held hers like magnets. 'Nevertheless,' he said silkily, 'you must be careful—especially after yesterday's faint. Perhaps you should try and get some sleep now.'

'It's mid-morning! And I'm perfectly all right——'

But Vittorio, his face glowering, had taken the hint. 'I shall not intrude any longer,' he said with cold formality.

'Oh, Vito—you're not intruding! Please don't go!'

Vito's expression was icy as he looked at her. 'His Excellency is right. You should rest now.'

'But when will I see you again?' she moaned unhappily.

'When I have time,' he said in a hard voice. The words shocked her, like a slap across the face.

'B—but I need you!'

'Do you?' Scorn glinted in his eyes as he looked from her to Cesare sitting beside her. 'Perhaps you will be so good as to give me a ring—when you are ready to come home.' He gave her a meaningful look.

'I will,' she promised miserably. 'Soon! Kiss me goodbye before you go,' she pleaded.

He leaned down without any warmth, and gave her the briefest of kisses on the cheek. Cesare was watching with an inner glitter, and she cursed him from the bottom of her heart.

'You can show yourself out, my dear chap?' he asked Vittorio languidly, without rising from beside Claudia.

'Of course.' He gave Cesare the slightest of bows, accompanied by a glare. His back was as stiff as a poker as he stalked out of the room.

As soon as the door closed, Claudia turned to Cesare with fierce green eyes. 'That was hateful,' she hissed.

'What was hateful?' he asked, arching one eyebrow in innocent enquiry.

'Touching me like that in front of him. Calling me *"carissima"*—and him "my dear chap". You had no right to send him away like that. You know exactly what he'll think! How will I ever make it up with him? I don't even know when I'll see him again!'

'Is he jealous? A village Othello?' He gave her a wickedly beautiful smile. 'You make a ravishing Desdemona, my dear—especially when your eyes blaze like that.'

'I don't like these games you play,' she said bitterly.

'Life is a game,' he smiled. He lifted her left hand, and studied it with brooding eyes 'Such a graceful hand. It should wear only the finest stones. That ring of Vittorio's was very much third-rate quality, I'm afraid.'

'It suited me fine,' she snapped.

His expression showed contempt. 'You should be more discriminating. About diamonds *and* men.' He lifted her hand to his mouth, and brushed her knuckles with warm lips. The touch made goose-flesh prickle all along her arm, and she watched in unwilling fascination as he turned her hand over and kissed her pulses, inhaling with arched nostrils.

'What is that scent?' he asked softly.

'Miss Dior,' she muttered.

'It suits you.'

'Vittorio's face was so unhappy,' she mourned. 'I

should have gone home with him today . . .'

'Forget Vittorio,' he commanded. 'This is where you belong.'

'It isn't. I ought to——'

'Rest,' he ordered firmly, silencing her with a finger on her lips. 'You ought to rest. Completely. And stop worrying.'

'How can I stop worrying? You're systematically ruining my life!'

He kissed the mutinous line of her mouth. 'Don't scowl,' he said softly. 'It makes your mouth irresistibly sexy.'

'You mustn't *say* things like that,' she cried exasperatedly. 'You can't just kiss me any time you feel like it! I'm an engaged woman, and my fiancé is upset enough as it is!'

'But kissing is natural.' He proved it by brushing her mouth with his again.

She pulled away angrily, but he wouldn't let her go. The more he kissed her, the more her lips seemed to cling to Cesare's, as though endowed with an amorous will of their own, and she felt that dismaying flicker of response inside her.

'Please,' she whispered shakily, 'don't do this . . .'

'Why not?' he asked. 'We both want it so badly.'

'You're doing this deliberately to humiliate me——'

'Nonsense.' His strong arms drew her close, his mouth plundering hers with expert, hungry kisses. Response flared in her.

God! Vittorio probably hadn't even left the palace yet, and she was melting in another man's arms like the most faithless of courtesans. It was crazy! Self-hate made her strain away from Cesare.

'No! *Please.*'

'Aren't you enjoying it?' he asked with a velvety

smile.

'*Enjoying* it?' she repeated bitterly. 'How can you be so amoral? This isn't a matter of enjoying or not enjoying. It's wrong, terribly wrong. You're making me into something ugly, something I don't want to be . . .'

'What?'

'A faithless woman!'

'Such bourgeois sentiments,' he mocked.

'I am bourgeois,' she said miserably. 'And I'm way out of my depth. I wish I'd never come here!'

'You had to come here,' he said forcefully. 'It was predestined, *carissima*. All this was meant to happen.'

'You're trying to make it sound like a grand passion,' she said with restless unhappiness. 'It can't be! It's just an infatuation!'

'An infatuation?' he growled.

'Yes! What else can it be?' Her nails were biting unconsciously into the hard muscles of his arms. 'I've known Vito for months. I've known you—*really* known you, I mean—for just a few days. It can only be an infatuation!'

His eyes were hard. 'Is that all it is for you?'

'Yes!' But she was as pale as death as she said the word. 'What sparked off these feelings, Cesare? After all, we knew each other for a couple of years without wanting to climb into bed together at the first opportunity. It all started when you saw me naked. Suddenly, you wanted me. You started kissing me, and I responded. But that's all it is—*sex*. It's just a physical attraction, intensified by proximity.' Defiantly, she looked up into his tanned face. 'What do you expect me to do, for heaven's sake? Stay here with you, and drift into a purely physical love affair that will be shallow and brief, and end with a broken heart for me?'

'That is not what I have in mind,' he said, tight-lipped. 'I want you sexually, yes. I've never wanted a woman more. But that is *not* all there is to it.' He trailed his lips down the arched line of her neck, making her shudder helplessly, and inhaled deeply at the scented hollow where her throat met her collar-bone. 'Your smell intoxicates me,' he whispered. 'You are like a musk-rose on a summer's day, all perfume and honeydew.'

She moaned softly, unable to stop her fingers from wandering through the crisp curls of his hair. 'Please stop,' she breathed. 'You are cruel to do this to me, Cesare . . .'

'Cruel?' he laughed softly. 'What an odd thing to say.' Cesare's mouth closed on hers with infinite ten-derness, the kiss making her float dizzily, as though on the warm waves of a southern sea. His hand strayed across her breasts, touching the erect peaks and making her gasp involuntarily. 'Is that cruel?'

She could only shake her head, her eyes telling him all too clearly how powerful her response to his caress was.

'You do not love Vittorio Brunelli,' he said quietly, looking down at her with deep grey eyes. 'He is a yokel, who only cares for the money you will bring him. You love Tuscany. Your only reason for agreeing to marry him was so that you could live here, among these vines and cypresses, under this sky that is always blue.'

'That's not true!' she whispered, her head spinning.

Cesare smiled, and kissed her yielding mouth. He rose from her bed, tall and dark, and frighteningly powerful over her. 'You will soon see,' he said implacably, 'whether it is true or not.'

CHAPTER SEVEN

VITO did not come to see her the next day. In her heart, Claudia hadn't really expected him to, but his absence affected her profoundly, none the less, as did not knowing when she would see him again. Was their engagement breaking up? He'd been almost a stranger to her last time. His eyes had been as cold as black stones. *When I have time.* The words had cut into her deeply.

She was having to face the possibility that, by buying that farm, she might have lost more than money. She might have irretrievably damaged her relationship with Vito Brunelli.

Curled up on her bed, staring at the gold angels that guarded its four corners, her mind was choked with thoughts that trudged round in endless circles.

What was she going to do? She had to face the truth some time or other. Even if she had been completely free of Vittorio, she doubted that she could ever have risked a casual affair with Cesare. He was the sort of man she could only love, not like, and the eventual parting from him would leave her broken-hearted.

Yet what possible future could there be between her and Cesare di Stefano? He obviously wanted her sexually, and his desire was intense. But how much more than that could there be? Despite his good intentions, his passion would fade, and in the end he would be satiated after a brief affair, throwing her over as soon as she began to bore him.

129

What had brought them together had not been mutual attraction, or any logical contact between their life-styles. It had been a mix-up over a farm overlooking Lucca, one of those strange coincidences, and nothing more.

And she hadn't got an inch further with Cesare about the farm all wekk. He simply refused to discuss it, laughing away her concerns, telling her it hardly mattered.

The awful thing was that she wasn't even particularly concerned about it any more, either. The farm, once to have been her and Vito's bridal home, had receded to the back of her mind, to rest among other problems that could be shelved until much, much later.

She only had one problem at the moment, which consumed all her thoughts. The problem posed by her own heart!

She and Cesare had come so close to making love, more than once over the past week. What would have happened if they had? And what would happen if the moment came again? It didn't bear thinking of. Already, she had done things that Vito must never know about.

If Vito could have seen her a bare hour before he'd arrived yesterday morning, her naked body wrapped in black silk, passionately returning the kiss of another man, he'd have gone mad on the spot.

Shame sent hot blood rushing to the skin of her cheeks and throat. It demeaned her. The force of her own response humiliated her. Was she so fickle that any other man could drive her fiancé from her thoughts?

Of course, Cesare was not any other man. He was unique. Yet that didn't make it one jot the better. That just raised other ugly questions.

If Vittorio Brunelli was so far from what she really wanted in a man, then did she really love him?

Could she still answer *yes* with automatic certainty? If she really loved Vittorio, then it ought to be impossible for Cesare to be able to do this to her. And if she *didn't* love Vittorio, then how could she ever go back to him?

The circles trudged round and round, and her eyes were bright with tears.

As he'd promised, Cesare took her to see his design studio and her worries about Vito were soon pushed to the back of her mind. She could never have believed that the Palazzo di Stefano could have housed a room like it.

It was, in fact, a suite of rooms at the back of the *palazzo*, overlooking the trees of the park. But it was completely different from the rest of the house. As she walked through, her light summer dress fluttering in the breeze from the open windows, she had the feeling of entering another world, a world that was as modern and avant-garde as the rest of the palace was classical.

The principal colours were black and white. On the walls and on several chrome tables were dozens of lights, some of them so futuristic that she could only stare at them. She guessed that they, like all the strange and striking collection of objects in the rooms, were Cesare's designs.

A collection of gleaming black pottery stood beside a sophisticated game involving stainless steel balls, which she had seen in all the big department stores. At the far end, a complex computer system had been set up on a huge desk, and another door opened into a second room, where she could see models and drawings on a long work-bench.

He followed her in, observing her wide-eyed stare with amusement. 'Well?' he asked.

'I'm flabbergasted.' She stroked a lamp that rose on three slender steel legs, like some futuristic robot. 'Is this all your work?'

'A tiny fraction of it.'

'You're a genius.'

He laughed gently, slipping his arm around her waist. But she could find no other word. The shapes and designs were incredible, showing a creative imagination that was bursting with life, and—like the man who had conceived them—virilely male. Leaning against him, she let him guide her through the bewildering variety of objects.

The black pottery fascinated her in particular. It was so sleek, the curved lines so sensual. She picked a big vase up, and caressed it in slender fingers. 'It's so black that it hardly even reflects,' she marvelled.

'A vanadium glaze,' he nodded. 'For a while that was almost my trademark. Then I got bored with it.'

'I know I've seen so many of these things before,' she said in awe. 'I've seen those lights in Harrods. And those chessmen, too. They're really popular. You're famous, Cesare!'

'As I said, most people don't give a damn who designs their possessions.' He shrugged. 'There's a designer cult in certain circles, of course. Trendy people insist on having sunglasses by this one, or jeans by that one. But I try to avoid that kind of thing. It's too limiting to be tied to the fashion of the hour. I have my own production company, so I'm able to dictate how and where the things I make are marketed.'

She'd been watching his face intently, but now she pounced on a foot-high brushed steel cone with a cry of delight. 'I've got one of these coffee-pots at home! And

I love it!'

'Indeed,' he smiled, looking unsurprised.

'It was damned expensive, but it was worth every penny. It never spills, it works like a dream, and it looks fabulous!' She was so pleased with the discovery that she kissed him impulsively on the mouth. 'I've had a Cesare di Stefano design in my own flat, and I never knew it.' She studied the familiar shape happily, remembering her pleasure when she'd bought her own. 'But mine has a different lip.'

'This is an early prototype. This one spills like mad,' he added. 'You'd be surprised at how much work goes into turning out a new coffee-pot. Things are easier since I got the computer.'

She glanced at the very expensive-looking system. 'Do you design things on the screen?'

'Yes. It's a CAD system. Computer-Aided Drafting,' he translated. 'Highly technical to use, but very powerful.'

'Show me,' she commanded in fascination.

He sat at the screen, and switched the machine on. She watched intently as his long, sure fingers moved a flat instrument across a grid-marked table, producing a line of light on the screen.

"This little thing is a digitiser. It sends messages into the computer to create three-dimensional images.' Under her eyes, the line of light on the screen was turning into an oval, starting to curl into the shape of a mask. Like magic, the mask acquired eyes, then a curved, smiling mouth. The nose was sketched out as a simple wedge, quickly refining into a realistic shape. Then the contours of the face were subtly shaded in.

She gasped as colour flooded the screen; a pale blue wash for the background, translucent skin that was almost life-like. The mouth was touched with pink, the eyes became a glowing green, acquiring dark pupils.

Before he even began to draw in the dark red hair, she'd recognised the face as her own.

'God,' she whispered, 'that's unbelievable!'

She stared as thick eyelashes were added to her eyes, the curve of her smile emphasised by the touch of a shadow. Another touch added a reflection to the glossy lips that almost looked as though they might be kissed.

'Want some make-up?' he smiled.

'Olive-green eye shadow,' she challenged, and watched in awe as the shading was expertly touched in.

'That's too dark,' he decided. The colour softened instantly. Her own face smiled back at her from the screen, etched in clear, intense colours. 'There. That's better. Do you like it?'

'I can hardly believe it. You've made me much too beautiful. But it's so lifelike, too—better than any photograph.'

'Most laymen have no idea that computers can do this kind of work,' he nodded, adding some finishing touches to the hair.

'It's you who've done the work, not the computer.' She looked into his eyes. 'You're an extraordinary man, Cesare.'

He smiled. 'I'll print it out.'

He typed in a command, and the big printer in the corner whirred into life.

'It'll take a few minutes to print out,' he said, rising. 'Come into the next room.'

She followed him. There was another surprise here. Filling one whole wall was a very large technical drawing. She recognised the sensual lines of the famous sports car immediately, and felt her eyes widen.

'Did you design *that?*'

'The shell, anyway,' he nodded.

'But that's—that's one of the most beautiful cars ever!'

'Thank you,' he nodded calmly. 'I'm glad you like it.'

'Like it?' She walked over to study it. 'I love it! I'd give a lot to own one of these!'

'You'd kill yourself,' he said drily.

'But all this means—you must be worth a fortune in your own right. I mean, apart from the palace and the title——'

He laughed as she came to a confused halt. 'How do you imagine this huge place stays in such good condition? How much do you imagine it costs to keep the grounds from turning into a wilderness, with today's costs? If I wasn't making a small fortune from my own work, Claudia, this estate would very soon eat itself up, the way noble estates have eaten themselves up all over Europe.' He came up behind her as she stared at the drawing, and slipped his arms round her waist, pulling her back against him. The touch of his hard body was thrilling, and she leaned her head back against his wide shoulder. 'Does it surprise you to learn that I am not an idle playboy?' he murmured, his mouth disturbingly close to her ear.

'I don't know what to say,' she admitted. 'How wrong can you be?'

She laid her hands lightly on his strong forearms. It touched something deep inside her to feel his strong arms around her waist. All she really wanted to do right now was turn round in the circle of Cesare's arms, put her own arms round his strong neck, and offer her mouth to be kissed . . .

Why did Vittorio never hold her like this?

It was as though he'd read her sudden thought.

'Does your Vito ever hold you in this way?' he asked quietly.

She closed her eyes. She was having to reconsider her blithe assumptions of yesterday morning very sharply. By now she had to face the fact that her response to Cesare was nothing to do with shock or tiredness.

Leaning against him like this, her head resting on his shoulder, she felt neither shocked nor tired. In fact, she had never felt more alive, more a woman, in her life.

'You don't answer,' he went on, brushing her neck with his lips. 'But you must know in your heart that he is not the man for you. You must know in your heart that this is where you belong, here with me—and not in some crumbling cottage with a man who is your inferior in every way.'

'Has anyone ever told you,' she said, trying to hide the tremble in her voice, 'that you're a terrible snob, Your Excellency?'

'A snob?' She sensed his smile. 'By my definition, a snob is one who thinks himself better than he really is. That is quite a different thing from knowing one's true worth. And you, my dearest Claudia, are the opposite of a snob. You intend to throw yourself away on someone who will never be worthy to kiss your shoes.'

'Vito's a good man,' she said restlessly.

'Good?' he retorted. 'What is that? Merely not bad. You are exceptional, *cara*. And you will only be happy with an exceptional man!'

She turned in his arms, and laid her finger on his lips. 'Please,' she whispered, 'please stop it! You make me so unhappy when you say such frightening things.'

'I must say them.' His eyes were deep, grey oceans that you could sink into and drown in. 'And the truth *is* sometimes frightening.'

'Can I really have been so wrong about Vito—and myself?'

'Men and women are foolish,' he smiled. 'To err, as they say, is human. I, for example, only discovered how much I cared for you by accident. Only that computer in there never makes a mistake.'

'But what if *you* are the one who is mistaken?' She searched the magnificent face with haunted eyes. 'Or worse—what if you're playing some cruel game with me?'

'Stay here with me,' he said in a velvety voice, 'and see whether I'm playing a game or not.'

'I can't stay here for ever,' she said dismally. 'It just isn't possible. Soon I'll have to go home with Vito.'

'No!' Cesare's dark brows came down like thunder. 'You and I have only just begun. You cannot go back to that fool.'

'You don't understand,' she said miserably. 'Life isn't the same for me as it is for you. You take life, like a piece of clay in your hands, and mould it exactly the way you want to. I can't do that. I have to muddle along like everyone else. I've got to bow to the pressures of my life—and Vito is a very big pressure in my life.'

'You?' he said in scorn. 'With your strong character and intelligent mind, to talk of pressure?'

'I don't have your character, or your mind,' she replied sadly. 'I'll settle for a lot less. And there are many kinds of love!'

'Are there?' he asked, tilting an ironic eyebrow.

'Yes. With you I feel great excitement, great happiness.' Now she was as red as she'd been pale a moment ago. 'I can't deny it. It's always been there. But that is just an accident.'

'An accident!'

'Yes. Call it chemistry. But it's a one-off thing. Vito may not be a dashing hero out of a film, but he is solid, dependable, reliable! He'll never let me down.'

'I wouldn't be so sure about that,' Cesare said grimly. 'Even if your fiancé were the paragon of reliability that you imagine him to be, is that all you ask for in a husband?'

'My life has been hard, Cesare. You once said that I saw Vito as a father-figure. Maybe there was more truth in that than you knew! I never had a father, and I need security out of life. I must have it. Vito gives it to me.'

'And I do not?'

'How can you?' she asked sadly. 'You are so brilliant, so talented, so creative. Your world is huge, filled with things and people who make demands on you. I don't mean that much to you.'

'Claudia!'

'Vito's world is narrow and limited,' she went on. 'I know that. But for that very reason, I mean much more to him. There won't be another woman for him. I can be absolutely sure that he'll never ever hurt me or abandon me.'

Cesare's fingers bit into her shoulders fiercely. 'He *will* hurt you,' he said sharply. 'You're fooling yourself. He will hurt you worse than you can possibly imagine, *cara.*'

She raised haunted eyes to his. 'I don't think he will,' she said in a low, trembling voice.

His eyes burned like coals. 'Vito holds you the way a boy holds a butterfly in his hands. For a moment he is spellbound by its beauty. Its very fragility awes him, making him hold his breath. But how long before he becomes a boy again, and his clumsy fingers close, and crush you?'

She shuddered, closing her eyes.

'That kind of security is an illusion,' he went on, less fiercely. 'It's a state of mind, not a real thing. Perhaps you were right,' he nodded. 'Perhaps our love *was* sparked off with my seeing your naked body. But a spark can never ignite a furnace unless there's a mountain of fuel there to start with! You and I have always been in love, but maybe we just never knew it. For myself, I give thanks to God that I found out before you married Vito Brunelli, and not after!' He touched her face. 'As for my losing interest in you—I could swear to you that I would never so much as look at another woman, that you will mean all the world to me. But it would be a waste of breath to make resounding declarations. All I can ask you to do—beg you to do—is stay with me long enough for me to prove how deeply I feel.'

'Oh, Cesare,' she whispered, her senses whirling.

He stared down at her with dark intensity.

'Don't go back to him,' he said quietly, making it a command that could not be disobeyed. 'Don't go back to him. And don't leave me.'

The next day, and the next, were among the most intense and unforgettable in Claudia's life.

It was not that she and Cesare did anything remarkably unusual together. After all, they did little but spend sun-baked hours in the sunny garden, walking and talking like lovers, as though nothing else existed but the need to know all about one another. No, it was some special quality in Cesare himself that brought this dizzily intense happiness to her.

It was partly in the way he touched her. He was a man who seemed to need to touch her all the time, slipping his arm round her waist, lacing his fingers through hers, kissing her with an intensity that made her senses reel. And she loved that, because she was the sort of woman who needed to be touched. Claudia was unashamedly physical, and she delighted in Cesare's answering physicality.

And the other half of it was the sense of togetherness that had existed between them from the start. With Vito, with all other men before him, she'd felt an incompleteness. If they matched her intellectually, then there was little or no physical attraction; if they were sexually alluring to her, then there was no mental contact.

But with Cesare, they were a perfect, seamless match. He was, quite simply, the cleverest and sexiest man she had ever known or dreamed of.

She had once thought Vito handsome; but Cesare was magnificent. She'd thought Vito intelligent; but Cesare was brilliant. And Vito's masculinity was immature and boyish beside the potency of Cesare's manhood.

He was, she had come to realise, the kind of man she had always dreamed of, so close to her ideal of manhood that he might have been made especially to conquer her from the moment of his birth. Sensual, brilliantly gifted, strong, sensitive, he was everything that made her heart quicken and her desire awaken.

That he had made what amounted to a declaration of love had filled her senses with fire. She was beginning to feel that their destinies must, after all, be entwined. But that thought brought as much anguish as it did joy.

It was a bakingly hot afternoon when they took two horses from the stables, and went riding. The grounds of the palace were immense, and after they had ridden round the edge of the glittering lake, admiring the façade of the great house, he led her along a track that stretched for long miles through woodland.

The tranquillity of the woods was immense. Hardly a sound disturbed the stillness, except the crunch of the horses' hooves among last year's dead leaves. Very occasionally, the distant chatter of a woodpecker could be heard, and once they twisted in their saddles to watch a solitary roe-deer start away from a thicket, high-kicking her way into the dappled depths of the wood.

They smiled instinctively at one another. For once, though, they were hardly talking. It was as though they didn't need to talk any more; Claudia had never felt such a deep peace in her heart, nor such a sense of completeness.

The air was aromatic with the scent of sun-baked pine needles. Wearing jeans and a light T-shirt, with a pair of boots that had been found for her in the tack-room, she hadn't felt this free and happy since her teens.

Building up Colefax & Brennan had been a long, hard struggle. She'd hardly been a teenager. While other girls of her age had been enjoying life, with boy-friends, parties and birthdays, she'd been working in the restaurant. When they had been courting and getting married, she'd been plunged in the intricacies of setting up an import business.

And even since her success, her engagement to Vito had effectively cut her off from the kind of social life another woman in her position might have chosen to enjoy.

These days with Cesare were like . . . Claudia hunted for the image. Like a precious refund from time. A giving-back of some of the happiness and freedom she'd sacrificed. If only they could last for ever!

After about an hour they reached a clearing in the very heart of the woods, where a stream trickled over mossy boulders. Here they dismounted. Tying the horses by the stream, they walked together in the dappled shade, Cesare's strong arm around her waist.

Wild flowers grew everywhere; wild box and gentians made vivid spots of yellow and blue among the russets and browns of fallen oak leaves, and the delicate spires of the wood-lily were everywhere. Claudia was so enchanted with a clump of pink cyclamens that Cesare stooped to pick her a little posy.

She examined the small, femininely sensual flowers with dreamy green eyes.

'I'm so happy, Cesare,' she said. 'God, I just wish this day would never end . . .'

'It doesn't have to end,' he said quietly.

She shook her head. 'Everything beautiful has to end.'

He smiled down at her, warm creases spreading at the corners of his eyes. 'Now, who gave you that piece of wisdom, *cara?*'

'It's a fact.' Her thoughts darkened as they turned to Vito. She leaned back against a tree, closing her eyes, and let her contemplations rush in.

Over the past days she been remorselessly approaching a moment of painful self-knowledge: that her love for Vito had been proved hollow.

She feared, deep in her heart, that she no longer loved him. Worse, she feared that, even if she had once felt passion for Vito, it had been engulfed and vaporised in the furnace of the feelings which Cesare di Stefano had ignited in her. Her heart was filled with a dark misgiving that she had nothing left to offer Vito any more . . .

And, if that was the truth, then for both their sakes their marriage could not go ahead.

This dream was coming to an end, swiftly. Now she must face her responsibilities, towards herself and towards Vito. Claudia had always taken her engagement seriously, as a thing in itself. It had not been mere form, a meaningless ceremony. She took it seriously even now, even though she suspected that she no longer loved—perhaps had never loved—Vito Brunelli.

Quite independently of what happened between her and Cesare, she knew that she must go back to Vito, and face the truth of her feelings for him. If she found that she no longer loved him—and she would find that out very soon—then she must cancel the engagement, formally and permanently.

All that was obviously impossible while she stayed here at the *palazzo*. She would never get her feelings straight about Vito while she was within the potent magnetism of Cesare's personality.

Nor could she help the feeling that her position was hardly a very creditable one while she remained here. She had managed to ignore it until now, but the realisation had come pressing in; it shamed her to contemplate cancelling her engagement while staying in her new lover's house. She knew how people would talk, and come to some humiliating conclusions about her character. The blow for Vito, too, would be crushings. Nothing could be more cruelly calculated to mortally wound his Italian pride. While she remained Cesare's house-guest, she would always be in an awkward position. She needed to get away, to clarify her own position, both to herself and to all observers.

And there was something else to think of, too. If she and Cesare were to become lovers, and enter a future together, then their start must be clean and clear. An old saying had been haunting her thoughts all day: *make sure you are off with the old love before you are on with the new*. She now knew what that proverb entailed.

For the sake of her own self-esteem, as well as for her and Cesare's love, they must start with a clean slate—with no attachments on either side, and no sense of guilt towards Vito. To start without a formal break from Vito would, she felt in her soul, be a bad omen for her and Cesare.

The inexorable conclusion was that she must return to Vito. She must leave this paradise for a short while, and do what had to be done. The idea filled her with pain, and a certain amount of dread. Leaving Cesare, and facing Vito with her doubts about their marriage, were going to be among of the hardest things she had ever done. But they had to be done, and she just prayed that Cesare would understand her reasons . . .

'Your thoughts must be very serious ones,' he said gently, touching her lips. 'What are they?'

She opened her eyes, and looked up at him dully. 'That I must soon leave here,' she answered.

His smile faded, and he slipped his arms round her waist, drawing her close against his hard chest and stomach. 'Why,' he whispered, 'must you be such an obstinate little fool?'

'I can't help the way I am. And I must go back to Vito.' Seeing the frightening glitter of anger in Cesare's eyes, she gave a little cry. 'I *must!* I can't stay here for ever, Cesare. I committed myself to Vittorio, and I owe him more than this.'

'What do you owe him?' he rasped.

'I owe it to him to behave honourably towards him,' she answered haltingly. 'You may have thrown my ring into the lake, Cesare, but it's not so easy to dispose of what that ring stood for.'

His arms tightened to the point of hurting her. 'You're talking of leaving me?' he demanded incredulously. 'Of going back to him—after all that has happened between us?'

'I owe it to him,' she repeated miserably. 'And I owe it to myself, too. I must see whether my love for him has really died.'

His eyes blazed. 'I see,' he said harshly.

'Do you see, I wonder?' she asked, looking up at him with dark eyes. 'You know that I feel a great deal for you, Cesare. But how can I be really sure of my feelings for you, unless I first make sure of my feelings for Vito?'

'I do not understand,' he retorted bitterly, 'how you can mention me and Vito in the same breath.'

'He's a man,' she smiled tiredly. 'The same as you. After all, I got engaged to him, didn't I? There must have been some sincere feelings in me. But I'll never know how I really feel about him while I'm close to you. You fill my mind, you stop me from seeing anything except you!'

He released her, and walked away from her, squatting by the pool to scoop up a handful of the crystal-clear water and splash his face, as though his skin were burning hot. She watched him with that old fascination; in such moments, his movements were like those of a tiger, smooth and vibrant with power. Even in the denims and cotton shirt, he carried an aura of glamorous male power about him.

He looked up at her, his face dripping, his passionate mouth set.

'No, Claudia,' he said in a rough voice. 'If you truly loved me, you would know it without having to go back to your Vito. You would feel it in your heart, the way I do, and you would need no further proof.'

'You obviously don't understand the way a woman's heart works,' she said with another pale smile. 'Even if I just go back to tell him it's all over, I must still go back! My love, try to understand! Would it make any difference if I said I was almost sure of my love, that I felt in my heart I would come back to you, soon?'

'No.' He rose to his feet, tall and dark. 'It is you who do not understand your own heart, Claudia.'

'But I must do what's honourable,' she pleaded.

'Honourable?' he snapped. She winced at the whiplash of scorn in his voice. 'You have a curious notion of honour. If you return to Vittorio Brunelli,' he went on, in the same fierce way, 'I will never forgive you.'

'Oh, don't say that!' Her eyes were glistening with tears suddenly. Unconsciously, she was crushing the poor cyclamens between her restless fingers. 'I must do what I think is right, Cesare. You're trying to force me to take a path that I cannot follow!'

'Claudia, listen to me.' He stepped up to her, his fingers biting painfully into her arms. 'Whatever else you may have found out over the past days, you must surely know by now that you do not love Vito. What necessity is there for you to go back?'

His eyes held hers for a long eternity, her emotions spinning in a maelstrom. Then she sagged wearily away from him. 'I must do it,' she whispered. 'I've decided.'

She let the limp petals fall to the earth around her boots, and stared at them unseeingly.

He remained where he was, watching her with intent eyes. 'If you leave me,' he said, his voice quiet and urgent, 'you will be making a most terrible mistake. And I mean it, Claudia. I will never forgive you.'

Without another word, he led her horse to her, and helped her to mount.

CHAPTER EIGHT

WHEN they got back to the *palazzo*, both silent and tense, there was a not altogether pleasant surprise awaiting them. Vito had arrived to see her half an hour earlier, and was waiting in the drawing-room.

Claudia's heart sank with a lurch as she realised that her resolutions had been brought to a grim and sudden reckoning. She was going to have to make her decision now, with no more time for prevarication or cowardice.

Vito's face was hard with anger as she greeted him, still wearing her riding clothes.

'The servants tell me you have been out riding all day,' he said in a rasping voice. 'I take it you are fully recovered, in that case.'

'Yes, I'm well,' she nodded, reaching for his hands. She made as much of a fuss of Vittorio as he would let her, perhaps because she felt she owed him more amends than he would ever know, but he was icy.

'It seems a pity to waste such a pleasant evening.' Cesare, who had come into the room behind her, was wearing an easy smile. 'Shall we sit out on the terrace?'

'That's a lovely idea,' she put in hastily, before Vito could refuse. As they walked out, though, she knew it was not going to be exactly a cosy party. Vito would want her to come home with him tonight, and she must obey. Despairingly, she was trying to strengthen her resolve for the parting, and praying that Cesare

147

would understand.

The three of them sat overlooking the golden-tinted lake, under the ripening vines, while a servant brought a tray of drinks.

'A glass of wine?' Cesare enquired, offering Vittorio a Chianti.

'As you please,' Vittorio said stiffly, accepting the drink.

'Excellent.' Cesare poured for them all. He plainly had no intention of leaving her and Vittorio alone together. 'Your very good healths.'

They drank in silence.

Vittorio put his empty glass down firmly, and turned to Cesare. 'My fiancée is resigning all claims to your farm,' he said with stiff formality, as though Claudia weren't there.

'What?' she blinked.

'There is no longer a problem,' he said with grim satisfaction. 'An acceptable arrangement has been reached with the Rossis.'

'Acceptable to whom?' Cesare asked silkily, while Claudia stared in surprise.

'Acceptable to my fiancée,' Vito replied.

'Even if she hasn't yet heard what the arrangement is?' Cesare enquired, raising one eyebrow. 'You assume a great deal, my friend.'

'Perhaps I do,' Vito said with suppressed anger. 'But then, I have the right. And since the matter no longer concerns *you*, Your Excellency, I would rather not discuss it in your presence. You will receive a letter from our solicitor in due course, setting out our position, and resigning any title to your land.' He turned to Claudia now. 'My mother has prepared a bedroom for you,' he said. His tone was peremptory. 'She is expecting you to come home with me tonight.'

It was said with a finality that left her in no doubt about what it was—an ultimatum. She glanced at his face unhappily. It was set and hard, the black eyes intense with emotion. It occurred to her that she still didn't have the faintest idea how she would explain her missing ring to him.

It came to her with leaden finality that she didn't really have any choice. For Vito's sake, for honour's sake, she must go home with him tonight. And she could not return to Cesare until she had faced the final break from Vito.

'You seem in a great hurry,' Cesare drawled, stretching out in his chair and glancing across at Vittorio. 'Don't you trust me with Claudia?'

'My fiancée has trespassed on your kindness too much already,' Vittorio said flatly. There was more than a little emphasis on the words 'my fiancée'. 'She has been here a week. You have been very kind, but now my family are quite capable of looking after her.'

Cesare raised a slow eyebrow. 'Indeed. But so am I. I really cannot see any necessity to rush her away tonight.'

'I am sure Claudia would be more comfortable among her own family,' Vito said woodenly. Claudia could almost see his hackles raising.

'And I am sure she would be more comfortable here,' Cesare retorted blandly. 'There is a great deal of room, as you can see, and no shortage of servants to take care of her. You have a large family, I understand.'

'Claudia always has her own room when she stays with us,' Vittorio replied stiffly. 'And my sisters will wait on her hand and foot, if that is what she wants. It may not be a palace, but she lacks for nothing.'

'How nice. But I doubt whether Claudia is quite well enough to travel yet.'

'She seems perfectly well to me,' Vito gritted, glancing at Claudia's slender legs. 'If she can spend the whole day on horseback, in this heat, I am sure she will survive the drive to Ferraro. In any case, if she feels at all unwell, our family doctor is quite competent to deal with the problem.'

'So is mine,' Cesare said smoothly. 'In fact, he is coming here tonight to check on Claudia's condition.'

'It would be better to put him off, then,' Vittorio retorted. 'Claudia has an appointment to see *our* doctor tonight, as well.'

'Oh, for heaven's sake!' The nervous exclamation burst out of her. 'There's no need to quarrel over me.' Both men were looking at her now, and she forced herself to go on. 'I am capable of making my own mind up. And I must go back with Vito.'

In the silence that followed, she glanced miserably at Cesare.

His eyes were on hers, deep and formidably intelligent. For a second, he seemed to be looking into her very soul, and she felt ready to burst into tears. He'd said he would never forgive her, and now she believed him.

Then it was as though shutters had come down behind his eyes, closing off his soul, and leaving only a mask. His mouth broke into one of those easy smiles that always seemed to make her heart turn over inside her.

'If that is what you want, *carissima,*' he said with perfect calm, 'then I will ask Anna to pack your possessions.'

Vittorio's expression was of keen, unmistakable triumph. 'My fiancée will be far happier among her own people,' he said meaningfully. 'But we are grateful to you for your help.' Claudia's heart twisted.

He turned back to her. 'There seems no point in delaying. Get ready now.'

A few words to the servant had the order transmitted. And then Cesare gestured at the scenery, as though nothing was more important. 'Is that not a beautiful sunset? Summer brings such wonderful skies.'

Claudia sat in a well of unhappiness that no beautiful sky could reach into. She felt in her heart that he did not understand her reasons for going back, and that she might, as he had predicted, have made a terrible mistake.

Her brief sojourn in paradise was over. In the space of a few seconds' talk, it had come to an end. It was as though Cesare's feelings for her had ceased, abruptly and for ever, the moment she'd agreed to go back with Vittorio.

And in that moment, he'd again become the mockingly smooth stranger of her first encounter. Gone for ever was the passionate lover who had thrown her fiancé's ring into his lake at dawn.

On the edge of tears, she wondered whether she would ever return here. Would she ever again know the feelings he had shown her—feelings of an intensity which had illuminated the past few days as though a new sun had dawned in her sky?

The thought of going back with Vito in her present mood, back to that crowded, inquisitive, noisy house, jarred on her nerves horribly.

Claudia looked at Vito, and tried to find the affection and trust she had once had for him. Some remnants of them must be there, somewhere. She could only hope that there was, and that he would allow her to break from him cleanly, and without pain, so that she could return to Cesare as quickly as possible. It was within his power to make her suffer as she had never suffered before.

Anna had materialised in the background to say that Claudia's clothes were packed. Vito's response was to stand up without ceremony. She had never noticed before how thick-set he was, how coarse-looking. She had once thought him rather elegant. But, beside Cesare's stallion-like grace, he was a plough-horse, dogged and uninspired.

'One other thing,' he said brusquely, his recent victories obviously giving him courage to face Cesare more boldly. 'My fiancée's ring. I would like to have it, please.'

'Then I hope you can swim, my dear fellow.' Cesare rose to his feet with a charming smile. 'Because it's at the bottom of the lake. A last Chianti before you go?'

Vittorio looked stuned, but Cesare's manner was so suave and pleasant that he seemed unable to frame another question. Claudia rose hastily, and turned to Cesare.

'Thank you,' she said, offering him her hand. 'You've been very kind to me. I won't forget—I won't forget any of it.'

'Not at all,' Cesare said easily, apparently oblivious to the fact that Claudia's green eyes were now swimming with tears. 'Take care of yourself, *cara.*'

'I hope—I hope we'll meet again,' she stammered, willing him to take her meaning. But he just shrugged slightly in reply.

With that old, easy charm, but not the slightest shred of warmth, he escorted the two of them down to the car. He was still pleasantly discussing trivia, as though she, and her stay here, hadn't meant a damned thing to him. As though a minor and rather troublesome guest was leaving, and that was all.

I'll never forgive you.

Could he really erase the past few days, pretend that the words he'd said to her had never been spoken?

She hadn't felt so utterly wretched in years. Grief was a huge pain in her heart, and parting from Cesare was like tearing something integral out of her body.

At the car, she tried to search for some special look in those beautiful grey eyes, some message that would tell her his feelings were still alive, that he would wait for her to come back to him.

But either it wasn't there, or her own eyes were too blinded by tears to see.

With a brief handshake and a few meaningless trivialities, it was over, and she was sitting next to Vito in the car, driving away into the night.

'Was he telling the truth? Did he throw the diamond into the lake?' Vito asked tautly as they joined the main road towards Ferraro.

She could only nod in silence.

Vito swore in dialect, and thumped the steering wheel with his fist. 'He will have to pay for it, damn him. That ring cost money. I knew it,' he added with a strange mixture of fury and exultation. 'I *knew* it!'

'What did you know?' she asked tiredly, trying to fight down the aching lump in her throat.

'Do you think I'm a fool?' he demanded with a harsh laugh. 'The man is crazy about you!'

She sat miserably, looking out of the window. 'Vito,' she began, 'there's a lot I have to explain to you——'

'You don't need to explain anything,' he said contemptuously. 'I saw it all, right from the first moment. I suppose he fascinated you, eh, with his aristocratic manners and his good looks? How far did you go with him?'

'There was nothing like that,' she said, more sharply.

He gave her a raking stare. 'You expect me to

believe you weren't his lover?'

'Of course I wasn't!' But she knew it was only true in a physical sense. Spiritually, she had never stopped making love to Cesare di Stefano from the moment she'd woken in his palace.

'Did he never try to kiss you? Never make overtures of any sort?'

'No,' she said in a small voice.

Vito snorted, but whether in disbelief or amusement she couldn't tell.

'What did you mean about the farm, and coming to an arrangement with the Rossis?' she asked, changing the subject.

'It was quite easy, as it happens, once we'd found the right approach.'

'The right approach?'

'We found a means of putting pressure on them.' He smiled without humour. 'I told you those people were crooks. My uncles have a friend who is an inspector of taxes in Pisa. They asked him to look into the Rossis' tax position. It didn't take him long to find certain anomalies, anomalies that would have cost Signor Rossi a great deal of money, and maybe even a year or two in jail. It was a simple matter to then talk him into making a refund. We agreed on four-fifths of the money.'

'I see,' she said dully.

He glanced at her angrily. 'You're not going to make difficulties now, for God's sake?'

'No,' she said tiredly. 'I'll do whatever you want, Vito.'

'You'd be well advised to,' he said meaningfully. 'I really cannot foresee any possible objections on your part, Claudia. In face, it astonishes me that you show no gratitude. I and my uncles have been working damned hard on your behalf, while you gratified yourself with your noble friend up there.'

'I am grateful,' she said with an effort. But nothing really mattered to her, and the whole affair with the farm now seemed to her a pointless and sordid exercise.

'I intend to invest that money for you,' he said meaningfully. 'Given your past performance, I rather feel I am better qualified to look after it than you are.'

He glanced at her, as if to gauge what effect his words had had. But she was too miserable to oppose him, and she just closed her eyes, lying back against the seat.

'Rest,' he said in satisfaction, taking her silence for assent. 'It's all over now, Claudia. All over.'

Claudia lay in the narrow bed, staring up at the dim ceiling. Though the church-tower bell had long since sounded midnight, sleep would not come. Satisfying the noisy curiosity of Vito's sisters about Cesare and the palace, over the blaring TV set that never went off, had drained her energy. It hadn't been pleasant to face Donna Maria's suspicious stare all evening, either. She knew that Vito's mother had never trusted her, and the atmosphere tonight had been very much one of 'I told you so'.

After the bliss of staying with Cesare, the confusion and tension of this crowded house had been like deliberate torture to her nerves. Even now, the television was on downstairs, a continuous murmur of music and metallic voices.

Was this, as Cesare had predicted, what the rest of her life would have been like? Her thoughts returned to him restlessly. He'd said she was making a terrible mistake. Maybe he'd been right.

God, she was missing him! She'd have given

anything for a touch of those gentle hands.

Would she ever see him again? It was a question that made her ache. Why had she ever left him? She might never be able to make him understand . . .

She knew the truth now. She no longer loved Vittorio Brunelli. Tonight, he had seemed like a stranger to her, and she had known with utter certainty that her feelings for him had changed for ever. She could no more think of spending her life with Vito than of putting it to an end.

She started as the door swung quietly open.

'Who's there?'

'Shhh.' Vito let himself silently into her little bedroom, and closed the door behind him. 'Were you awake?'

'Yes.' She sank back on the bed. 'I couldn't sleep. I should have taken that camomile your mother made me.'

'You've had an exciting time of it,' he said, with a dry note in his voice. In the near-darkness she could see that he was wearing his dressing-gown. 'This place must seem very humble after what you've been used to. But now you're back. You're back where you belong.'

'Yes,' she nodded. 'I'm back.'

His voice took on a note of contempt. 'That man may be rich, but he probably hasn't done a day's honest work in his life.' She thought about that studio full of briliant designs, but said nothing. Vito was probably happier with his illusions than he would have been with the truth.

He reached out to stroke her hair. 'We Brunellis may not have blue blood or a palace, but we know how to make money, girl. You'll see, when I'm in charge of your business, I'll make us rich. Rich,' he repeated softly. His hand slid down to cup her breast.

The gesture was so startling that she froze for a moment, then turned away to avoid his grasping hand.

'Vito, no.'

'You're so soft,' he muttered. To her dismay, he was reaching for her breasts again, his fingers ungentle. 'Come on! Are you shy?'

'Vito,' she protested unhappily, 'I'm tired!'

'Too tired for me,' he said grimly. 'But not too tired for his lordship at the palace.'

'It's rather late for this kind of argument, isn't it?' she asked wearily.

'No, it's not too late!' He sounded savage. 'Do you think I'm blind? He threw your engagement ring into the lake! If he wasn't a duke, I'd kill him for that!'

'That kind of talk is ugly,' she snapped. The way he loomed so threateningly over her was horrible. 'Why don't you go back to your bed? We'll talk in the morning.'

'I could see what you were up to,' he gritted. 'It was in your face, clear as a scarlet letter on your forehead. Lying in his bed with next to nothing on. You've always been fascinated by him. You used to talk about him for hours. Do you expect me to believe he never tried to possess you?'

'Whether he tried or not,' she said tensely, 'he didn't actually do it.'

'You are a good liar, girl.'

Tiredly, she sat up to face him. 'That's a cruel thing to say!'

'You have lied to me about many things.'

'Such as?'

'You're not a virgin,' he said with brutal force.

'Nor are you,' she shot back.

'It's different for a man!' She could see his eyes gleam in the darkness. 'You let me believe you were a virgin!'

'I never made any claims either way,' she reminded him drily. 'And why is it different for a man?'

'Because it is,' he said in a savage voice. 'I suppose you've had a dozen lovers? Two dozen?'

'Don't be obscene,' she sighed, sagging back against the pillows. 'I only had one. He was a man I broke up with two years before I even met you.'

'If you could do it once, you could do it a dozen times! And you expect me to believe that you virtuously turned a man like Cesare di Stefano down, when he came to your bed?'

'Yes,' she said sharply, 'I do! If I'd made love with Cesare, I would have told you, Vito.'

'Liar!' he repeated. Suddenly, he was furious. 'When I think of the way I worshipped you,' he gritted, 'I could laugh at myself. I hardly dared touch you. I thought you so pure! And yet, somehow, I knew what you were really like, underneath the virginal exterior. Mamma warned me, and I didn't listen.'

'Vito!'

'Oh, don't worry,' he sneered. 'I don't find that sort of thing unattractive. Maybe I even like girls like you, girls who know what a man wants. What I don't like is your hypocrisy.'

'All right,' she said tensely, too hurt to keep silent. 'You want to know the truth? The truth is that I've fallen in love with him, Vito.'

'Bitch!' he snorted.

She took a shaky breath. 'And I came back with you tonight for one reason. To break off our engagement, honourably.'

'Honourably?' His eyes were blazing in the darkness. 'You think I'm going to let you humiliate me in front of the whole town?'

'There's no question of humiliation,' she said unsteadily. 'We'll simply announce that our engagement is over, by mutual decision.'

'And then you'll go back to di Stefano?' His voice quivered. 'Over my dead body!'

'You can't stop me,' she said sadly. 'Whether Cesare will have me back or not, our engagement has to end. I didn't want to talk about it now, at night. But you've forced me . . .'

'Very well!' With unexpected violence, he was on top of her, crushing her back against the bed. 'Go, if you want to,' he said roughly. 'And may you rot. But first, I want some of what every other man seems to be getting!'

He kissed her hard on the mouth, trying to force his tongue through her clenched teeth, while his hands squeezed at her breasts. The animal violence of the assault stunned her for a few seconds, then she fought away furiously, and swung away from him.

'You've been drinking,' she gasped, her mouth filled with the taste of the whisky he'd drunk.

'Yes,' he nodded fiercely. 'I've been drinking gall. It tastes very bitter, Claudia. Maybe the taste of your flesh will take its bitterness off my tongue.'

This time she couldn't get away from him. He was brutally strong, pinning her down with his body as he kissed her mouth, crushing her lips against her teeth. She fought desperately, but his hands were everywhere, grabbing at her breasts, trying to thrust between her thighs. She clawed at his back, suddenly hating him enough to want to really hurt. He muttered an obscenity, then laughed.

'We should have done this a long time ago,' he said thickly. 'My uncles were right. You wouldn't have gone running after di Stefano then.' Using his knee cruelly, Vito pushed her thighs apart. 'I'll show you, girl. I'll show you that I'm more of a man than any decadent aristocrat——'

She squirmed frantically away, and swung her palm at his face. He struck back instantly, the blow rattling her teeth in her head, so that stars exploded in her eyes.

'Get out of here,' she sobbed. *'Get out!'*

The bedroom door flew open, and light flooded the room. Donna Maria stood in the doorway, her broad face stiff with astonishment at the sight that met her eyes. Claudia's nightgown had been torn in the struggle, showing the curve of one breast, and her long, naked legs were splayed across the sheet. A touch of crimson at her mouth showed where Vito's blow had cut her lip.

Donna Maria's eyes blazed at Claudia. 'Whore,' she shouted. 'I knew it from the first! Haven't you done enough?'

Vito pulled his dressing-gown closed over his own nakedness, and rose to his feet.

'I am sorry, Mamma,' he said in a husky voice. 'I didn't know what I was doing. She tempted me.'

'It was an evil day when you first laid those green eyes of yours on my son,' Donna Maria said fiercely. 'You are not good enough for him. Go back to your own kind, Claudia. There is no place for you here!'

Sobbing, Claudia swung out of bed, and ran to the cupboard.

'What are you doing?' Vito demanded.

'Getting my clothes,' she said tightly, and touched the cut on her mouth. 'I'm going *now.*'

'You can't,' he said impatiently, and grasped her arms with hard fingers. 'Be reasonable.'

Passion gave her strength to swing nails at his face in a blow which, if it had landed, would have drawn blood, and he jumped back in alarm. 'Get *away* from me,' she said shakily. 'Don't you ever *touch* me again, Vito.' He stared at her blankly, and she turned back to the cupboard, blindly yanking out clothes.

'Leave her.' Donna Maria's voice was like a rusty gate closing. 'Let her go, Vittorio. She was never meant for you.' Using her considerable strength, she pushed her son out of the room, and closed the door on Claudia.

Oblivious to them, Claudia was already dressing. Tears of pain and fury streamed down her face. How dared he? How dared they both treat her like that? Her breasts were aching from Vito's grabbing fingers, and her lip was already swelling hotly. No one had ever called her a whore, or treated her like one, in her life. What a horrible mistake it had all been. Had she really imagined she could marry into this family?

She hadn't the faintest idea where she would go, or what she would do. She only knew that she must get out of this house now, for ever.

She couldn't be bothered to hunt for all her clothes among the Brunelli possessions that cluttered the cupboard. What she stood up in would suffice. She had to get out of here now. The thought was suddenly there. Yes, out of this house, and back to Cesare.

She pulled on whatever first came to hand, and stepped into a pair of shoes. She found a lightweight fawn coat on a hanger. Hers or one of the girls? It didn't matter. She'd send it back if it wasn't hers. She slung it over her shoulders, then, scooping all the small things that were hers into her handbag, she went to the mirror to brush her hair.

Her appearance shocked her; she was as white as a sheet, the cut on her mouth all too evident. It didn't matter. She pulled the door open, and walked quickly down the stairs.

Two of Vito's sisters were watching from their bedroom door, wide-eyed and silent. And Vito himself was standing against the front door. His face was very pale and set, and he barred her way.

'Claudia,' he said tautly, 'you cannot go like this. It's nearly one o'clock. You have nowhere to go to.'

'You're wrong,' she said, her body still shaking with passion. 'Let me pass, Vito.'

'I'm sorry,' he said helplessly. 'I—I don't know what came over me, girl. I think—I think I went a little mad. Please let me try and make it up to you, please!'

'It's over, Vito,' she said in a voice that hardly sounded like her own. 'Your mother is right. I was never meant for you.'

'I love you,' he said, his lips trembling. 'You cannot go like this. I love you!'

'You wouldn't have done and said those things tonight if you loved me,' she said bitterly. 'You've never understood the first thing about me. And it's taken me until tonight to understand you.'

'Claudia!'

Before he could go on, Donna Maria's voice came from the top of the stairs. 'Let her go, my son! She's a witch! She would poison your life!'

'That's right.' Claudia didn't even bother turning round. 'I'm a witch, Vito. Let me pass.'

When he didn't move, she simply pushed him aside. Like a straw man, his body moved limply away from the door, and she swung it open. The night air was cold on her face.

She heard Vito cry out her name, and then she slammed the door shut behind her, and walked out into the deserted street.

No one came after her. The little town was dark and

silent. Claudia walked swiftly towards the centre, where she knew there was a phone booth. There was still so much pain and anger in her slim body that she positively vibrated with it. How dared he? After all they'd been to each other, to grope at her body like that, saying such horrible things, to hit her——

What a complete fool she'd been. Cesare was right; she'd known next to nothing about Vito, and he'd known even less about her. They had never been suited, right from the start. Pray God that she hadn't irrevocably damaged her relationship with Cesare.

She saw the phone booth, and walked into it. She put a coin into the machine, and dialled the number of the *palazzo*. Everyone would be asleep by now, but this was an emergency.

The male voice which answered was strange to her.

'It's Claudia Brennan,' she said, still slightly breathless. 'Can I speak to the Duke, please?'

'I'm afraid that His Excellency is not in residence.'

'What?' She felt a blank chill descend on her. 'I don't understand. He must be in residence!'

'I'm sorry, *signorina,* but he is not.'

'But—but he was there only a few hours ago! I saw him myself at seven this evening——'

'His Excellency is not here.' The tone was slightly harder now.

Despairingly, Claudia slumped against the cold glass. 'Can you tell me where he has gone to, then?'

'I am not at liberty to give out that information.'

'When will he be back, then?'

'I cannot say, *signorina.*'

She felt pain spread through her heart. He couldn't have gone anywhere. Not at this hour of night. He must simply not want to speak to her. Her punishment for having left with Vito. 'Please,' she said unsteadily, 'this is very urgent. Can you get a message to His Excellency for me?'

The answer was decidedly cold. 'I cannot accept any urgent message, *signorina*. I have no idea when His Excellency will return, and he has made no arrangements for messages to be passed on to him.'

'Then how can I get in touch with him?' she asked desperately.

'I suggest you contact His Excellency's offices in Florence. His secretary may be able to help you.'

'But—but I need to speak to him *now*.'

'I must repeat, *signorina,* that the Duke is not in residence——'

'You're lying,' she said fiercely. This was a cruel and horrible game they were playing with her. 'He cannot possibly have left. He had no plans to go anywhere. He just won't speak to me, will he? He left orders that my calls weren't to be put through, and you're too afraid to wake him!'

There was a silence on the line. And she heard the deep voice in her mind. *I will never forgive you, Claudia.*

'Oh,' she exclaimed bitterly, 'never mind. To hell with you—*and* him.'

She slammed the receiver down on to the cradle, and pounded her fist senselessly against the wall, her eyes flooding with tears of unbearable hurt.

CHAPTER NINE

AUTUMN had brought with it a season of cold mist and prematurely falling leaves. The big lime tree outside the Highbury Grove shop was shedding like yellow rain every time the wind blew round the corner, and Claudia had been glad to put the central heating on for the first time that year.

'That's better.' Mrs Garraway, the manageress, peeled the pink cardigan off her imposing bust, and subsided back behind the electronic cash register. 'I expect you'll be glad to get off to sunny Italy this November, Miss Brennan.'

'Hmmm?' Claudia looked up vaguely from Vito's letter. 'November?'

'I say, you'll be glad to get away from all this.' Mrs Garraway nodded her permed head at the weather outside, then at the envelope Claudia was holding, with its Italian stamps. 'You are going on a trip this November, as usual?'

'Oh.' Claudia shook her head. 'No. I won't be going back until the New Year. This isn't business —it's from my fiancé.' She corrected herself. 'My ex-fiancé.'

In fact, the letter was a bare account of how some outstanding financial details between them had been resolved. At the end there was an almost casual note:

I'm sure you will be pleased to hear that I am getting married in January, to Eleonora Moni, the daughter of Bruno the butcher.

Her smile was wry. For a few weeks after she'd left, Vito had sent her long letters filled with despair. His grief over their parting seemed to have settled down remarkably quickly. No doubt his redoubtable Mamma had had a hand in that. Bruno Moni was a rich man by village standards, and she had a vague memory of a pretty, vivacious girl behind the counter.

So Vito was getting married. The thought just didn't affect her, one way or the other. And once she'd been convinced that he was the only man for her. One of these days she would get a little parcel containing some sugared almonds tied up in a scrap of net, a symbolic hint of the marriage-feast that had taken place in Ferraro, and she knew she would feel just what she felt now—that it was news from strangers.

Mrs Garraway was watching Claudia's face quizzically. 'Not having second thoughts, are you?'

'About getting married?' Claudia smiled wryly, her soft mouth turning down bitterly at the corners. 'No, Mrs Garraway, I'm not. He's found someone else, and in any case, I'm quite cured of *that* bug.'

'Ah. I thought you looked sad for a moment there.' Mrs Garraway, a widow, liked to take a motherly interest in Claudia's love-life. 'When I lost my Ernest, I used to swear I'd never get married again. One good man was enough for me, that's what I used to say. But the years roll by, Miss Brennan, and the years never come back. If I were to meet the right sort of man again——'

She interrupted herself to rise majestically from behind the cash register to attend to a customer, and Claudia slipped with gratitude into the stock-room. Why was it that everyone seemed to think they had the right to give her advice?

God, she was just glad to be out of that misery, and

back to the humdrum world of practical things. Like attending to the little barred window in the back of the shop.

She eyed it thoughtfully. There had been a burglary at this shop while she was in Italy, and though the glass had been repaired, and the bars re-fitted, the local crime prevention officer had advised her that a steel shutter would be a better solution. She'd had a look at the estimates, and had more or less decided to get shutters fitted to the back windows of both her shops before the bad weather started in earnest.

Picking up the telephone, she called the security company, and arranged for the work to be started that weekend.

Then she mooched round the shelves, with the computer stock printout in her hand. With the approach of Christmas, sales were predictably starting to soar, especially of the more expensive wines, liqueurs and whiskies. She would have to do some ordering this afternoon.

And, given that she hadn't been able to face a return visit to Tuscany this autumn, she was going to have to do some telephoning to Italy as well. Though she also sold French and German wines, as well as spirits, Chiantis were still the main feature of the Colefax & Brennan line. It was not unknown for her better customers to buy several cases at Christmas, and despite her large reserves it would be disastrous to risk running low.

Better leave that till much later, however, because nobody did business much before four o'clock, Italian time. Right now, they'd be too busy eating, sleeping, and making love.

The sudden memory of Cesare hit her like a stone wall, making her sway giddily. For a moment she thought she'd have to sit down. The smell of summer was all around her, the feel of his arms, the smell of his hair . . .

Would she never forget his touch, his eyes? She leaned miserably against the steel shelving, her mind floded with vivid memories.

As always, her thoughts turned from Cesare to the memory of that ghastly night in Ferraro, when she'd stormed out of Vito's house into the deserted streets. She could never think of Cesare without thinking of that ordeal.

He'd said he would never forgive her for leaving him. Well, she would never forgive him for not coming to her in her hour of need. When she'd been desperate for his help and comfort, he'd just turned his back on her.

How could he have just refused to come, after a call like that, in the middle of the night? His pride might have been hurt, yes; but, for all he knew, she might have been in terrible trouble.

As it was, it had been awful enough. She hadn't been able to raise a taxi at that hour, and to walk the ten miles to Pisa, back to the Splendid, was unthinkable in the darkness, especially wearing the light shoes that were all she had. Going back to the Brunelli household was equally out of the question.

In the end she'd walked to the Church of San Felipe. It was open, and she had let herself into the vast darkness, lit only by the handful of guttering votary candles near the altar. She'd spent one of the most miserable nights of her life there, curled up on a hard pew, too upset to sleep. Her brain had been seething with her woes, injustices and sufferings. She'd finally dropped off near dawn, only to be woken shortly afterwards by a worried sacristan come to prepare the altar for matins.

At six she'd got the early morning bus to Pisa, in the company of curiously staring factory workers and farm labourers. On the long ride back to Pisa that bright morning, and in the weeks that followed, Claudia had had plenty of time to think things through.

The lesson was painfully obvious. Trust no one but yourself.

She'd learned early on in life that most people were simply out for what they could get. Any pretence to the contrary just disguised a more cunning and rapacious nature than usual. Vito and Cesare had both fooled her, in different ways. But Cesare's betrayal had been the worst.

Vito had the excuse of his background, his inability to understand someone like her. After all, his fault had lain mainly in thinking her something she was not, just as she, too, had entertained illusions about him. He would be happier with his Eleonora than he ever could have been with her.

But Cesare, the aristocrat, who had thrilled her soul with words of love, who had deliberately set out to make her love him, had no such excuse. How often had he claimed to be able to understand her fully? Had he not sworn that his feelings for her ran deep and true?

Yet what kind of love was it that could turn a deaf ear to a cry for help in the night?

In that cruel refusal she clearly saw the arrogant, hard di Stefano face, staring out at the world with its heavy-lidded gaze, unforgiving of any lapse, swift to avenge any wrong.

With a sigh, Claudia forced herself to get back to work. There had been a long period when she'd been waiting for a word from Cesare, some kind of explanation or apology. But it hadn't ever come.

As the weeks drifted past, the candle of hope in her heart had flickered and died, and had long since grown as cold as death. There hadn't been any mistake. There hadn't been any misunderstanding.

He had promised that he would not forgive her, and that was how it was. As cut and dried as the figures in the stock-list she was now staring at, her eyes wet with unshed tears.

'I meant to tell you, Miss Brennan.' Mrs Gerraway had popped her head round the door, and either hadn't seen, or was diplomatically ignoring, Claudia's swimming eyes. 'A man was calling for you this morning, a Mr George Handel. I've written his number down here. He wanted you to call him back some time today.'

'Thanks, Mrs Garraway.' Claudia took the note, making an effort to smile, and set about trying to stitch up the ragged edges of her day.

It wasn't until lunch time that she remembered about her mystery caller, and rang him back; and when she did so, it was to get a surprise.

'Ah, Miss Brennan, how nice of you to call back.' The voice was articulate and pleasant, professionally so. 'I'm George Handel of BBC Television's *Fine Food, Fine Wines* programme. I don't know if you ever watch the show.'

'Of course I do,' Claudia said, damning herself for not recognising the name, and the rubicund, bespectacled face it conjured up. 'Every Tuesday without fail. What can I do for you, Mr Handel?'

'I'd very much like you to come on the show on the twenty-seventh of next month,' came the prompt reply. 'We're planning a two-part special on Chianti wines, and you're obviously one of the people we want to hear from. As you know, the show is broadcast live in front of a studio audience. How does the idea strike you?'

'I'm staggered,' she said honestly. 'You do realise that I'm just a minor businesswoman, and very far from a real expert on Chianti?'

'Oh, there'll be heavyweights on the programme, too,' he assured her. 'But we're aiming at a well-balanced show with broad appeal. It's all a matter of chemistry, isn't it? Putting together a pudding with the right ingredients. Our viewers tend to be on the under-forty side, and my producer and I feel certain that you can make a valid contribution.'

'Especially if I wear a low-cut dress?' some imp prompted her to suggest in a sweet voice.

'I have seen photographs of you in the press, and the answer is yes,' came the unhesitating reply. 'How would you like to come to Pebble Mill and talk the whole thing over with us?'

'I'd love to,' she decided instinctively. It was a long time since anything remotely exciting had happened to her! When would you like to see me?'

'As soon as possible. You name a time.'

'Friday at eleven?'

'My secretary's writing that down now,' George Handel replied in his unhesitating way. 'I look forward to seeing you, Miss Brennan. Goodbye.'

'Bye.'

Claudia sat staring at the window, just enjoying the sensation of depression lifting from her heart. There was nothing like a little bit of attention for lifting you out of the doldrums! How lovely to have people wanting you, eager to talk to you. It was like getting a peep of blue skies through a prison window!

She was just only beginning to realise quite how miserably unhappy she had been since leaving Italy. Maybe this was an omen. A sign to her to start trying to enjoy life a little more?

The meeting with George Handel and his producer, a handsome, middle-aged woman named Pat Stafford, was extremely cordial. Claudia knew perfectly well that the two media people were weighing her up in terms of presentability and capacity to be boring or nervous on set, but that didn't bother her. It was just the sort of challenge she enjoyed.

The programme they outlined to her over mid-morning tea in George's office sounded like fun, too. She would be one of a 'panel' of tasters, two of whom would be people from the audience, and she would be expected to make some judgement about a selection of Chianti wines.

That would be followed by a recorded sequence which had been filmed in Italy earlier in the year by George himself, showing the Tuscan countryside and the grape harvest.

Later in the programme, she'd have a short spot to herself, in which she would recommend a dozen or so Chiantis of her own choice, describing the characteristics of each.

That was the real plum, her chance to shine, and that it was being offered at all was very flattering.

To a businesswoman, the publicity involved for Colefax & Brennan was very tempting. But to a bright, outgoing person who enjoyed attention, it was irresistible. The more George and Pat described it, the more exciting the prospect sounded. Appearing on a popular television wine programme! What better antidote could there be to post-Cesare blues?

'I think it's all shaping up very smoothly,' Pat Stafford said at last, rising from her chair. 'I'm going to leave you and George to talk things through, because I'm due at a producer's conference in five minutes. It was a pleasure meeting you, Claudia. See you again soon.'

After she had left, George checked his heavy gold Rolex. 'I'm an early luncher,' he announced, patting his ample stomach. 'Rossetti's do a very nice *spaghetti alle. vongole* on a Friday. It's just around the corner. Care to join me?'

'I'd love to,' Claudia smiled.

Over the spaghetti, which was just as delicious as George had claimed it would be, the television presenter did a little discreet name-dropping. That was a weakness of TV people in general, she knew, but a harmless one.

Claudia made sure she was suitably impressed with the catalogue of politicians he golfed with and celebrities whose yachts he had sailed on.

But she nearly choked on a clam when George added, 'And of course, I'm a great friend of *your* great friend, Cesare di Stefano.'

'Cesare?' she said faintly, mopping her mouth with the napkin.

'In *fact*,' George went on, 'now that I come to think of it, I first heard your name through Cesare. He thinks very highly of you.'

'Does he?' Trying to look natural, Claudia took a swallow of wine to wash the reluctant shellfish down. 'When—when did you last see Cesare di Stefano?'

'In August, while we were shooting that documentary about the harvest. Several of his vineyards feature in it, as it happens. There's even a shot of the *palazzo*. By golly, isn't that a fantastic place? But I don't need to tell you that, of course. He mentioned that you'd spent a week or two there.'

Comparing dates revealed that George must have arrived within a fortnight of her departure. They reminisced about the beauty of the house and grounds for a while.

'That'll all be in your backyard soon,' George concluded. 'You're getting married to an Italian, aren't you?'

'No.'

'Oh?' George looked interested. 'Cesare told me that you were engaged to a local man. An accountant, I think he said. He seemed quite sure about it.'

'I *was* engaged,' Claudia said briefly. 'I'm not any more.'

'Oh? Sorry to hear that. You must have broken up rather suddenly. Cesare didn't seem to have heard about it.'

'Cesare is obviously not as informed about my life as he should be,' Claudia said drily.

George picked up the nuance, but evidently didn't know quite what to make of it. 'He's a remarkable man, don't you think?'

'Oh, yes,' she nodded, resuming her meal. 'He's that, all right.'

'Cesare is the handsomest man I know,' George went on, 'and one of the most cultured. Have you seen any of the things he's designed?'

She nodded. 'He's very gifted.'

'Oh, unquestionably.' He sent her a sly look from behind his heavy hornrims, which were obviously carefully cultivated as part of his screen image. She wondered whether he really wore the bulky, uncomfortable-looking things in private. 'He gave me the distinct impression that he has a very soft spot for *you*.'

She didn't answer, and George didn't press the point, passing lightly on to other topics.

But Claudia's mind had been snagged on a phrase of George's. *Cesare evidently hadn't heard.* Was that true?

She'd always assumed that Cesare must know by now that she and Vito were no longer together. But why should she have made that assumption?

Supposing he didn't know; supposing that all this time he had been under the impression that she and Vito were still due to get married?

God!

'What's the matter?' George asked in concern. 'You've gone as white as a sheet. Here, have another glass of wine! Are you all right?'

'I'm fine,' she said, as composedly as she could. But she was shivering deep inside. That thought had come like a thunderbolt, and the blood had drained from her face.

'You're not allergic to seafood, are you?' George asked, peering at her suspiciously. 'I took a girl out once and fed her on prawns. She came out in this terrible strawberry rash within half an hour. I had to rush her to the hospital——'

'I'm fine,' she repeated, wishing for God's sake that George would just stop talking. 'I just felt a bit faint for a moment. Maybe I'm getting a cold. I hate this winter weather.' She rubbed her face, which always went numb when she'd had a shock. Why had she never thought of that in all these weeks? Why had it taken George Handel's careless remark to make it occur to her? A burning restlessness seemed to have possessed her. She pushed her plate away. 'I'm sorry, George, my appetite's gone. Do you mind if I don't finish my *vongole?*'

'Avoid them like the plague, dear girl,' he urged,

still peering at her skin as though expecting the straw-berry rash at any moment. 'Have an ice-cream instead. Or would you prefer an antihistamine?'

'I'll just go straight on to coffee,' she decided with a faint smile. 'Tell me more about your stay with Cesare.'

'Loved every minute of it. That man really under-stands what hospitality means. Those wines of his are jolly good, as you know, and as for the female company . . .' George sighed reminiscently as he mopped up his sauce with a piece of bread.

'The female company?' Claudia asked in puzzle-ment.

'Stunning.' George's eyes were glowing distantly. 'What a lot of beautiful women he knows. And all supposed to be *contessas* and *baronessas* and what have you. The swimming pool was like Hollywood every afternoon. I've never seen such small bikinis.' He chuckled fatly. 'Talk about taste! His personal choice was a raver called Mariuccia della Something-or-other. God, what a figure! Hair like golden silk, right down to her bottom, and eyes like . . .'

At that moment, George caught Claudia's own eyes, which were the glacial green of a polar iceberg, and he tailed off suddenly.

'Oh,' he said awkwardly. 'Am I being terribly indiscreet?'

'You're being terribly interesting,' Claudia rasped, in a tone that made him wince. 'You were describing Signorina della Something-or-other's eyes.'

'Of course, half of these females,' George said, trying to gain ground, like a man scrambling back over a cliff edge, 'were his relations. Second and third cousins and so on. In fact, I'm positive that this Marriuccia was a relation, too——'

'Are you?' Claudia was sitting very stiffly, hands clenched in her lap.

George puffed out his pink cheeks. 'I get the impression I *have* been indiscreet,' he said. Getting no encouragement from Claudia's frozen face, he sighed. 'They used to call me Blabbermouth at school, you know. Cesare is not going to be pleased with me, I fear. So there *is* something between the two of you? You should at least have *hinted*. I mean, I did fish for a clue, didn't I? You sort of gave the impression that . . .' He sagged back, defeated by the heavy silence. 'Look, if I've given you the idea that there was a continual orgy going on, that's very far from the case, I mean, you know what a good family man he is. He just had this house-party of young cousins at the time I was there. I mean, the man was quite fatherly towards them.'

'The thought of Cesare being fatherly with a bevy of beautiful young girls in bikinis is one which takes some swallowing,' Claudia enunciated frostily.

So much for her sudden rush to the head! While she'd been crying her heart out every night in London, broken-hearted and missing him with every shred of her being, Cesare had been installing hot-and cold-running dolly-birds in every room.

Damn him to hell! Was that what his promises of eternal devotion had meant? That within weeks of her departure he would be working his way through the female aristocracy of Italy? The thought was sickening, infuriating!

'Oh, dear,' George sighed, following the expressions which were crossing Claudia's face. 'Will you do me a favour, dear?'

'Try me,' she invited, lips pressed together hard.

'When you *do* get around to skinning him, don't tell

him I told you. Please?'

'I have no intention of doing anything to him,' she said thinly. 'I don't expect I'll ever see him again during the whole rest of my life.'

'Not even when he arrives next week?'

'Next week?' Claudia repeated, her frozen expression changing to one of astonishment.

George shook his head in bafflement. '*Are* you having something with him or aren't you? Yes, he's arriving in London next week. Monday, I think. For the big exhibition. Selfridge's. *You* know.'

'No,' Claudia said numbly, 'I don't.'

'You *don't?*' George stared at her for a long moment, evidently utterly at sea. 'They're holding an exhibition of his designs at Selfridge's. It's to launch that male fashion business. Cesare's going to be there for the opening. He's only staying a few days. I mean, for heaven's sake, didn't you know? Didn't he *tell* you?'

'No,' she said, in an even smaller voice. 'I didn't know a thing about it.'

'Well, I'm glad that the light of battle has faded from your eye, dear. But if you'll permit me to say so, you are a very mysterious young person *indeed.*'

Every fibre of her soul called her to go and see Cesare as soon as he arrived. It was a need like that of a drug addict's craving, a hunger to see him that tormented her continually, from the moment George Handel had told her he was coming.

Yet her mind told her otherwise. Her mind told her she'd already had one lucky escape from Cesare di Stefano, reminded her of the way he'd turned his back on her in her hour of need. Her mind tortured her with imaginings of silken-haired Mariuccias, bikini-clad and languorously draped around a sun-bronzed Cesare, who cared not a fig whether Claudia Brennan lived or died.

But her heart whispered other things. That she might have been mistaken about him. That silly George Handel might have exaggerated. That Cesare might not know that she was free.

The weekend was a desert of indecision and nerves. On Saturday morning, accidentally on purpose, she passed through Selfridge's. The exhibition was well advertised. It was coinciding with the launch of a new range of menswear, toiletries and jewellery, all bearing the di Stefano name. There was a stunningly brooding photograph of Cesare on all the posters and, behind a row of canvas screens, she glimpsed overalled men carrying various objects in glistening black and stainless steel. With a sharp pang she recognised the black pottery she'd so adored at the *palazzo*. She fled from the store, her nerves tingling.

She took her mother to the pictures on Saturday evening, and on Sunday morning, a day of bright, cold sunshine, she went to the Highbury Grove shop to open up for the workmen to install the steel shutter.

Sitting huddled in her greatcoat, making regular cups of tea for the two flirtatious young fitters, she was no nearer an answer than she had been on Friday.

'You ain't 'arf got some lovely stuff in 'ere,' the cheekier of the two hinted, eyeing the shelves of wine. 'That brew in the wicker basket's Chianti, ain't it? Yeh, thought so. Don't fancy letting us try a bottle or two, Miss Brennan?'

'That depends on how good a job you do,' she smiled. 'In the meantime, it's strictly tea.'

She returned to her thoughts. Cesare was only staying for a few days, according to George.

Well? Was she going to make contact with him, or not?

The question was made all the sharper by the knowledge, deep inside, that if she didn't get in touch with him during these precious few days, she might well never see Cesare again. If there was any chance that her own feelings were still the same, and that his feelings had not changed either, then she must grasp it now, before it was for ever too late.

As to his feelings, she had no way of telling. She might as well try and guess the other side of the moon.

But, for her own feelings, there really wasn't any doubt at all. There hadn't ever been any doubt.

She had loved him almost from the first, and had never stopped loving him. All this time, in her silent, pent-up rage against him, she had only been fooling herself. There would never be another man to take Cesare's place in her heart. There would never be another love to take the place of the love she felt for him.

By the time the fitters had finished, and the handsome new shutter was in place, Claudia's mind was made up. She must make contact. She had no choice. But not directly.

George had told her he would be staying at the Ritz —where else?—and she would leave a message for him at reception, asking him to call her. If he wanted to follow it up, then she would be waiting. If not——

She shivered as she locked up the shop. If not, it was going to be a cold, cold winter.

'What a lovely bit of stuff, eh, Charlie?'

The appreciative comment drifted up the street to her from the van, where the fitters were packing up. She knew they weren't referring to the bottle of Chianti she had given them apiece, and a smile crept across her mouth. There was just a chance that Cesare had found her as difficult to forget as she had found him!

She called the Ritz as soon as she got back home, and left a very simple message for Cesare—just her name and number. She got the distinct impression that hers wasn't the only breathless message that would be awaiting Cesare's arrival.

She sat by the phone for a while, looking at the sunset and dreaming of those Tuscan days. Maybe she'd open a bottle of Chianti herself over dinner, the better to dream on . . .

She made herself a light meal, had two glasses of wine, and curled up on the settee. The heating had been on and it was deliciously warm in the flat, and she was very soon in the land of her dreams.

It was late when she awoke, still unsure where she was. Her mind was far away, under a blue sky.

The sound that had woken her came again, the insistent ding-dong of her front door bell.

Her heart was pounding as she jerked awake, and a soaring, unreasonable hope sent her speeding along the passage to fling the door open.

He was there. Tall, darkly tanned by English standards, he was wearing a beautiful grey overcoat and a white silk scarf, and he looked like a star, a king! He looked down at her with that slow, amused smile. Claudia's heart stopped dead for a second as the grey eyes met hers, and she felt her face turn pale.

'*Cesare!* You—you're not arriving until tomorrow night!'

The idiotic words were the first that came to her paralysed lips, and he tilted one ironic eyebrow.

'My mistake,' he said gently. 'I'll go back where I

came from.'

'*No!*' she yelped as he made a half-turn to leave. 'No! Silly George Handel's mistake. He told me you weren't due until tomorrow.'

'I arrived an hour ago.'

She couldn't hide the joy that flickered in her green eyes. 'Then—then you must have come here as soon as you got my message!'

'My bags are still unpacked,' he agreed with a slight smile. 'Or shouldn't I be so obvious?'

'Oh, Cesare!' Suddenly she threw her arms round his neck, her face pressed tight against his chest as she clung to him. He held her in strong arms, one hand caressing her hair.

'God,' she whimpered, 'I've missed you so much . . .'

'I've never stopped thinking about you,' he replied. 'I wanted to see you very badly, Claudia. I'd hoped there would be a message from you . . .' With an effort, he pushed her away. 'However, this is not very clever of us. Touching you is having a terrible effect on my heart-rate.'

'I was hoping . . .' Claudia didn't finish the sentence. Instead, she drew a very shaky breath, and tried to smile. Seeing him in the flesh, after having thought of nothing else for days, had been a shock, and she'd started trembling like a leaf in reaction. He was so incredibly handsome!

'I don't think much of your climate,' he said pointedly. 'I've been standing out here ringing your doorbell for ten minutes. Is it any warmer indoors?'

'Sorry! I've been asleep,' she apologised breathlessly, ushering him in. Her fingers were shaking so much that she could hardly fasten the latch, and he watched with inscrutable eyes as she fumbled helplessly

with the mechanism, gabbling on like a schoolgirl.
'Damn this thing! It's supposed to be burglar-proof . . .
the crime-rate is appalling round here . . . I've had a
steel shutter installed at the shop today——'

'That sounds like you,' he said with a dry note.
'Shall I do that for you?'

'Yes, please,' she begged, surrendering with relief.
'It's one of those silly safety things that intruders can't
open. There, you've done it.'

'Steel shutters and safety-locks,' he said, turning to
her. 'Are you still guarding that tender heart of yours?'

'No. Not any more.'

They faced each other in the narrow hallway, just
staring at each other with hungry eyes.

'You look well,' she whispered.

'So do you,' he said quietly. His eyes were travelling
over every inch of her. She was aching to reach out to
him again, but she didn't dare. There was too much
emotion between them.

She hadn't noticed that he was carrying a large,
expensive-looking flat box under his arm. He gave it to
her now, and she lifted the lid. Under the rustling
tissue-paper was something made out of the finest
black silk, covered with tiny metallic flowers . . .

'Oh, Cesare!' She shook the gown out, and held it
up. The impeccable lines were evident, the mastery of
the cutting. 'It's magnificent!'

'I had it made by the best fashion house in
Florence.' He showed her the label, and smiled wryly
at her shining eyes. 'I was hoping you would wear it to
come to this affair at Selfridge's with me.'

'You know I will!'

'Good. And how is dear Vito?' he asked with a hint
of bitterness. And then she knew.

'You haven't heard, have you?' she said huskily,

holding the gown to her breast and staring up at him with adoring eyes.

'Heard what?' he asked, shaking his dark head.

'About me and Vito.' And as he continued to stare at her, his grey eyes narrowed intently, she leaned against the wall, still hugging the silk dress. 'Can't you guess?'

She saw his tanned face turn pale, and for a moment he seemed to sway. 'Are you telling me it's over between you?'

'It's been over for months! It was over the night I left you.'

'What are you talking about?' he whispered, his eyes burning.

Claudia laughed weakly. 'Why did you refuse to speak to me that night, when I called?'

'Because I wasn't there!'

'You *really* weren't there?'

'Of course I really wasn't there,' he repeated impatiently. 'Don't play with me, Claudia, for God's sake. What happened between you and Vito that night?'

'Would you like a cup of tea?'

'No! I want to know——'

'Or would you prefer coffee'

'Claudia,' he groaned, 'what the hell are you talking about?'

'Have you tried these almond biscuits?' she enquired sweetly.

He stared at her as though she were mad, then she saw the memory creep back into his eyes. He smiled, but he still hadn't recovered his poise. 'I suppose I deserve to have my own weapons thrown back at me. Did you think I was refusing to talk to you that night?'

'I thought . . .' She shook her head. Now was not

the time to tell him what she'd thought that night, and since. 'Where were you, as a matter of interest?'

'On my way to Sicily.'

'To *Sicily?*' she echoed.

'I have a villa in Taormina.' He gave her a wry look. 'Do we have to discuss all this in the hallway?'

She took him into the lounge, and helped him off with his greatcoat. Underneath it he was wearing a beautiful grey suit, elegant as only he could be.

She curled up beside him on the sofa, and looked at him dreamily. Her man. The only man she would ever love. 'Tell me about that night,' she commanded softly. 'It's important to me.'

He reached for her hand. 'After you left, the *palazzo* seemed hateful to me. It was exactly what you once called it—a morgue, inhabited only by the echo of your laughter, and the ruins of our love.' His fingers tightened around hers. 'I didn't know whether I would ever see you again.'

'But I said I would come back to you!'

'You said you *might* come back,' he reminded her. 'I had a terrible feeling you would decide to stay with Vito—for the security you said he gave you. I couldn't bear it there any longer. So I packed a bag, got in the Ferrari, and drove straight down to Sicily overnight.'

The joy inside her was like a wave, threatening to spill over. 'That must have been quite a drive,' she said solemnly.

'It was fast,' he agreed with a dry smile. Their eyes met. In those grey depths, Claudia suddenly saw what she'd prayed she would see—that deep, passionate love for her, the love that matched her own. It was there, she knew it. She could feel it in every muscle of the big, male body, could hear it in the deep, soft voice. He loved her. He had never stopped loving her, just as she had never stopped loving him.

Weakness washed over her, and it was an effort to control herself.

'Did you never wonder what that call in the night was all about?'

'Of course,' he said, still watching her with that intent frown. 'The servants rang me in Sicily the next day to tell me about it. They said you had been very upset, almost abusive. I called Vittorio Brunelli at once for an explanation.'

'And what did he say?' she enquired.

'I didn't speak to him. One of his sisters answered. She laughed off my anxiety. She told me that you and Vito had quarrelled in the night, and that you'd both been a little drunk, but that you'd patched the argument up by then.'

'Well, well,' Claudia mused in admiration.

'When I asked to speak to you, she told me that you were still asleep in bed.' Cesare's face tightened. 'With her brother.'

'Hah!' she snorted. 'In that house? A likely story! And about—our marriage?'

'She told me you were planning to marry near Christmas,' Cesare said quietly. 'It did not occur to me to question that this was the truth.'

Claudia sat in silence, seeing the scene in her mind's eye. The nervous sister, feigning amusement on the phone; Vito crouching next to her, still hoping against hope that it would all come right in the end, whispering the lies she was to pass on to Cesare. She could almost feel his desperate anxiety to stop her from going back to Cesare di Stefano, his need to cover up what had happened.

That was why he had never contacted her. It dawned on her that, all this time, he too must have been suffering the torments of the damned. But, unlike her, he had been able to assuage some of the pain——

She reached out to unfasten his tie. 'And so,' she crooned, fingers busy with the silken knot, 'all these months, you've been licking your wounds with Mariuccia of the long, blonde hair, by the poolside?'

'You've been talking to George Handel,' he said, unblinking.

'Yes.' Her perfect white teeth bared in a grin, Claudia wound the red silk tie round his strong neck, and clenched the ends in her fists. 'Should I strangle you now? Or later?'

He caught her hands in his own, a smile dawning in his eyes. 'George has a determinedly dirty mind. Mariuccia is my cousin. The relationship is purely platonic, I assure you. Do you really think that the hurt you caused me could have been taken away by some kind of sexual orgy?'

Her face softened. 'Did I hurt you?' she asked with misty eyes.

'More than I believed possible. Stop strangling me, Claudia. Was that girl lying to me that night?'

'Through her teeth.'

'Then tell me, for God's sake,' he said urgently, 'what you were really doing that night!'

She smiled back into his eyes. 'Until dawn I was sitting in the Church of San Felipe, built by your ancestor in 1493, and surrounded by the crypts of twenty generations of di Stefanos.'

His dark brows came down like thunder. 'What the hell were you doing in the church all night? he demanded.

'Thinking about you.' She shook her head, too full to speak about that. 'It hardly matters any more. Vito and I broke up that night, my love. I have never seen

him since then. If you don't believe me, a few days ago
I had a letter from him saying that he was getting
married to the butcher's daughter.' She shook her
head, her mouth trembling. 'I've been sitting here for
months,' she said, trying to hold back the tears, 'thinking that you didn't care about me, that you'd forgotten
me . . .'

'Claudia!' He was crushing her in his arms, covering her face with kisses. 'For God's sake, don't cry,' he
whispered. 'The time for crying is over, for ever! If I'd
known you were waiting for me, do you think I
wouldn't have flown to you in a second? Why didn't
you call me, why didn't you *tell* me?

'God knows! I once thought you capable of murder-
ing me,' she said, clinging to him tightly. 'Perhaps I'm
much, much stupider than you can ever imagine, my
love. Forgive me, forgive me!'

'Forgive *me,*' he said huskily. 'Forgive me for having
been stupid enough to believe that your love wasn't
real. God! Why did I ever let you go? I *knew* it was a
terrible mistake!'

'Oh, Cesare, don't ever leave me again, not ever!'

'Leave you?' He laughed tenderly, and kissed the
tears away from her lids. 'Not for the world, *carissima*. I
let you go once—I'll never let you go again!'

'Tell me that you love me.'

'I love you,' he said gently, his mouth close to hers.
'And I knew in my heart that you loved me. It's a gift
of the di Stefanos, remember? But I loved you long
before you loved me.'

'Not true!' she contradicted him softly. 'I can't
remember a time when I didn't love you! Now tell me
that you're going to marry me.'

'I'm going to marry you,' he smiled, 'as soon as we
can get a special licence. We have a lot of lost time to

make up for. Oh, my love, think of how mad we've been!'

'No,' she smiled, snuggling into his arms. 'I'm going to think about the future, instead. I'm yours, Cesare, every scrap of me. I'll never leave you for a moment.'

'I'm not Vito,' he reminded her with a laugh. 'I want you to stay fulfilled, with your own career——'

'My career!' She wound her arms round him, and settled herself into his lap. He cradled her in his arms, laughing. Staring up into his face, she felt a happiness deeper and stronger than anything she'd ever known, a happiness that would never fade and die, but would grow brighter and stronger with the passing years. 'When we get back to Tuscany, I'll go and see old Ugo Zanoletti, and start writing that book,' she smiled. 'A woman has to have *some* kind of work. But as for my career—you are going to be my career,' she whispered, 'my life, my everything. I'm going to become a Cesare di Stefano specialist. Someone else can run Colefax & Brennan from now on. From now on, I intend to devote the rest of my life to becoming a connoisseur of your love.'

'That sounds a splendid idea,' he purred, his lips closing on hers. 'Shall we try the vintage now? Or should we wait for that special licence?'

'We've wasted enough time.' Ruthlessly, she dug her nails into his strong shoulders, and drew him down. 'Let's start *now*.'

Coming Next Month

Available in April wherever paperback books are sold, or through
Harlequin Reader Service:

In the U.S.
901 Fuhrmann Blvd.
P.O. Box 1397
Buffalo, N.Y. 14240-1397

In Canada
P.O. Box 603
Fort Erie, Ontario
L2A 5X3

This April, don't miss Harlequin's new Award of
Excellence title from

Harlequin Presents...

CAROLE
MORTIMER

Award of Excellence

elusive as the unicorn

*When Eve Eden discovered that Adam
Gardener, successful art entrepreneur, was
searching for the legendary English artist, The
Unicorn, she nervously shied away. The Unicorn's
true identity hit too close to home....*

*Besides, Eve was rattled by Adam's
mesmerizing presence, especially in the light
of the ridiculous coincidence of their names—
and his determination to take advantage of it!
But Eve was already engaged to marry her
longtime friend, Paul.*

*Yet Eve found herself troubled by the different
choices Adam and Paul presented. If only the
answer to her dilemma didn't keep eluding her....*

HP1258-1